Love's Second Chance

SAPPHIC SECOND CHANCES

SAPPHIC SHELLEY

Introduction

Love's Second Act

Time has a way of changing everything, but can it mend what was once broken? As two women reunite after years of silence, they must decide if love can bloom again amidst the remnants of their shared past.

In the bustling city of Riverbend, former lovers Ava and Jamie find themselves crossing paths again at a mutual friend's wedding. Once a passionate couple, their love was stifled by fear and circumstance, leaving them with unresolved feelings. As they navigate the complexities of their new lives—Ava as a successful playwright and Jamie as a devoted teacher—they must confront the choices that tore them apart. In a story filled with laughter, tears, and the possibility of redemption, can they embrace love's second act and reclaim the happiness they once shared?

One

THE THEATER LOBBY buzzed with anticipation, a symphony of excited voices rising above the sea of well-dressed patrons. Ava stepped through the glass doors, her emerald green dress shimmering under the soft glow of the chandeliers. The scent of buttered popcorn wafted through the air, mingling with the faint aroma of expensive perfume.

Ava's heart pounded in her chest as she scanned the crowd, searching for familiar faces amidst the sea of strangers. Whispers of her name floated by - "That's Ava Sinclair, the playwright" - sending a thrill down her spine. Her gaze lingered on the elegant posters adorning the walls, bold letters proclaiming the world premiere of her latest work.

She moved through the throng of people, the silk of

her dress caressing her skin with each step. Snippets of conversations drifted past her ears:

"I've heard it's her most daring play yet."

"The advance reviews are glowing. A masterpiece, they say."

Pride swelled in Ava's chest, yet a flicker of doubt lingered in the shadows of her thoughts. Would they see the truth woven between the lines, the pieces of her heart laid bare on the stage?

A gentle touch on her arm pulled Ava from her reverie. "Ava, darling! You look ravishing," a velvety voice purred. She turned to see Victoria, her agent, resplendent in a sleek black gown.

"Thank you, Victoria," Ava replied, a smile playing at the corners of her lips. "I can hardly believe this moment has arrived."

"Believe it, my dear. Your talent is undeniable." Victoria leaned in closer, her eyes gleaming with mischief. "And I've heard whispers of a certain someone in attendance tonight. Perhaps a reunion is on the horizon?"

Ava's heart stuttered, images of Jamie flooding her mind unbidden. The softness of her touch, the intensity of her gaze, the bittersweet tang of unspoken goodbyes.

She swallowed hard, her voice barely above a whisper. "Perhaps. But the past has a way of haunting the present."

Victoria squeezed her arm, a knowing smile on her lips. "The stage is set, Ava. Let the magic unfold."

With a deep breath, Ava turned back to the crowd, her eyes scanning the sea of faces once more. Tonight, her truth would be laid bare, and the ghosts of her past would dance in the spotlight. The curtain was about to rise, and Ava knew that everything was about to change.

As the lights dimmed and the audience settled into their seats, Ava found her own spot in the theater, her heart fluttering with a mix of nerves and excitement. The velvet upholstery of the chair cradled her body, but it did little to soothe the whirlwind of emotions that swirled within her. She closed her eyes for a moment, inhaling deeply, the scent of perfume and anticipation mingling in the air.

The murmur of the crowd faded into a hushed silence, and Ava's pulse quickened, knowing that her words, her soul, were about to come to life on stage. She gripped the armrests, her fingertips sinking into the plush fabric, as if anchoring herself to the present moment.

A soft rustling drew her attention, and Ava turned her head to see a figure settling into the seat beside her. In the dim light, she caught a glimpse of a profile, the curve of a cheek, the glint of an earring. Her breath caught in her throat, and she whispered, "Jamie?"

The figure turned, of course it wasn't Jamie. Ava always found herself searching for Jamie's eyes in every crowd. Jamie, whose haunting eyes, pools of blue, had once held the promise of forever. A small smile tugged at Jamie's lips, a silent acknowledgment of the unspoken history between them.

Ava could fantazise Jamie murmuring, "Hella, Ava," her voice soft and rich, like honey drizzling over Ava's skin. "I couldn't miss your big night."

Ava's heart swelled, a bittersweet ache blossoming in her chest. The years melted away, and for a fleeting moment, she was transported back to a time when love was a force that consumed her, a fire that burned with an intensity she feared would never be rekindled.

"I'm glad you're here," Ava whispered to her her imagined partner, her voice trembling slightly. She reached out, imagining her fingers brushing against Jamie's hand, a featherlight touch that ignited a thousand memories.

She brushed note seat rest, dreaming of Jamie's fingers curled around hers, a gentle squeeze that spoke volumes. "Me too, Ava. Me too."

The theater darkened, and the stage illuminated, bathing the room in a soft glow. Ava's attention was drawn to the unfolding scene, her own words echoing in the air, but the imagined warmth of Jamie's hand in hers remained a constant presence, a tether to a past that refused to be forgotten.

As the play progressed, Ava found herself lost in the emotions of the characters, her own experiences bleeding into the dialogue, the unspoken longing, the ache of missed opportunities. She fantasized Jamie's gaze upon her, a silent witness to the raw vulnerability that poured from her soul.

In that moment, surrounded by the artistry of her own creation and the presence of the woman who had once held her heart, Ava felt a glimmer of hope, a whisper of possibility. Perhaps the ghosts of her past were not meant to haunt her, but rather to guide her towards a future where love could be rewritten, where the pages of their story could be filled with new chapters, new beginnings.

The stage lights danced, casting shadows and illuminating truths, and Ava knew that this night would be a turning point, a chance to confront the unresolved and embrace the unknown. Imagining Jamie by her side, she felt a strength she had long forgotten, a resilience that had been forged in the fires of heartbreak and tempered by the passage of time.

As the curtain fell on the first act, Ava turned, pretending to see Jamie, her eyes shining with a mix of tears and wonder. "Thank you for being here," she whispered, her voice raw with emotion. "Thank you for seeing me."

Ava told herself it was alright to dream: Jamie smiled, a genuine, heartfelt smile that warmed Ava from within. "I've always seen you, Ava. And I always will."

* * *

As the intermission lights brightened the theater, Jamie wasn't there. Ava slipped away from the bustling crowd, her heart heavy with the weight of memories. She navigated the winding corridors, her footsteps echoing against the polished floors, until she found herself in a quiet corner, a sanctuary amidst the chaos.

With trembling hands, she reached for her phone, unlocking the screen to reveal a gallery of moments frozen in time. Each photograph told a story, a chapter in the novel of her life, and as she scrolled through the images, the bittersweet ache in her chest grew stronger.

There, in the soft glow of the screen, was a candid shot of Jamie, her hazel eyes crinkled with laughter, her curly brown hair tousled by a gentle breeze. Ava's finger hovered over the image, tracing the contours of Jamie's face, remembering the warmth of her touch, the melody of her voice.

Another swipe, and a new memory emerged—a stolen moment captured in pixels, two hands intertwined, a promise of forever etched in the spaces between their fingers. Ava's heart clenched, a pang of longing so acute that it stole her breath away.

As she lost herself in the labyrinth of memories, Ava felt the weight of the years press down upon her, the ghosts of her past whispering in the shadows. Each photograph was a reminder of what had been, of the love that had consumed her, of the dreams that had shattered like glass upon the ground.

And yet, amidst the pain, there was a flicker of hope, a tiny ember that refused to be extinguished. For in the depths of those hazel eyes, in the curve of that gentle smile, Ava saw a reflection of her own soul, a mirrored longing that spoke of second chances and unfinished stories.

With a shaky breath, Ava closed her eyes, allowing the memories to wash over her, to fill the cracks in her heart with the golden light of possibility. She knew that the path ahead was uncertain, that the wounds of the past would not heal overnight, but in that moment, she dared to believe in the power of love, in the strength of her own resilience.

As the intermission drew to a close, Ava tucked her phone away, a bittersweet smile tugging at her lips. She straightened her shoulders, ready to face the world once more, armed with the knowledge that the ghosts of her past did not define her future.

With purposeful strides, she made her way back to the theater, back to the stage where her words had come to life, back to the woman who held the key to her heart. And as the curtain rose once more, Ava felt a renewed sense of hope, a quiet determination to rewrite the ending of her own story, to create a masterpiece of love and redemption, one scene at a time.

* * *

The house lights dimmed, and a hush fell over the audience as Ava settled into her seat, her fingers gripping the playbill with a mixture of anticipation and trepidation. The stage, bathed in a soft, ethereal glow, beckoned her, drawing her into a world of her own creation, a world where the lines between fiction and reality blurred.

As the actors took their places, Ava's heart began to race, each beat a reminder of the unresolved tension that simmered beneath the surface of her carefully crafted words. The opening lines of the second act washed over her, the cadence of the dialogue a siren's song, luring her deeper into the emotional tapestry she had woven.

With each passing scene, Ava found herself leaning forward, her eyes fixed upon the stage, her breath catching in her throat as the characters navigated the treacherous waters of love and loss. The raw vulnerability displayed by the actors was a mirror of her own, a reflection of the scars she carried, the wounds that had never fully healed.

As the play reached its climax, Ava's grip on the armrests tightened, her knuckles turning white with the intensity of her emotions. The final scene unfolded before her, a dance of passion and pain, of unspoken desires and the weight of regret. In the lead actress's eyes, Ava saw a flicker of Jamie's spirit, a ghost of the love they had once shared, now immortalized upon the stage.

The air grew heavy with the weight of the moment, the theater crackling with an energy that was palpable, electric. Ava's heart pounded in her chest, a drumbeat of anticipation, as the final lines were spoken, the words a whispered prayer, a plea for forgiveness and understanding.

As the curtain fell, Ava released a breath she hadn't realized she'd been holding, her eyes shimmering with unshed tears. The applause that erupted around her was a distant echo, drowned out by the pounding of her own heart, the rush of blood in her ears.

In that moment, Ava knew that the play was more than just a story, more than just a work of art. It was a testament to the power of love, to the resilience of the human spirit, to the hope that even the most shattered hearts could be mended, piece by precious piece.

Rising from her seat, Ava joined the standing ovation, her hands coming together in a rhythmic applause that reverberated through the theater. The pride she felt for her work, for the raw emotion that had been poured into every line, every scene, was overwhelming. And yet, beneath the surface of her triumph, a profound longing persisted, a yearning for the one person who could truly understand the depths of her creation.

* * *

As the audience began to filter out of the theater, Ava lingered, her eyes scanning the lobby, searching for a familiar face among the sea of admirers. Friends and colleagues approached her, their faces alight with praise and congratulations, their words a blur of superlatives and accolades.

"Ava, darling, that was absolutely breathtaking," a fellow playwright gushed, clasping her hands in admiration. "The way you captured the essence of love, the pain of loss... it was simply divine."

Ava smiled graciously, her lips curving into a practiced expression of gratitude. "Thank you, that means the world to me," she replied, her voice soft, almost distant.

As the well-wishers continued to surround her, Ava's mind drifted, the conversations fading into a hazy background noise. Her thoughts were consumed by Jamie, by the memories of stolen glances and gentle touches, of whispered confessions and the bittersweet ache of love unfulfilled.

She moved through the lobby as if in a dream, her body present but her soul adrift, lost in the labyrinth of her own heart. The scent of Jamie's perfume seemed to linger in the air, a phantom fragrance that haunted her senses, a reminder of the void that had never been filled.

Ava's fingers absently traced the delicate chain around

her neck, the one that held the small, golden locket Jamie had given her on their first anniversary. Inside, a tiny photograph of the two of them, forever frozen in a moment of pure, unadulterated happiness, a testament to the love they had once shared.

As the last of the theatergoers dispersed, Ava found herself alone in the lobby, the silence a heavy cloak that settled over her shoulders. She gazed at the posters that adorned the walls, her own name emblazoned across them in bold, elegant script, a symbol of her success, her triumph.

And yet, in that moment, the accolades felt hollow, the praise a bitter reminder of the one thing she truly desired, the one person who could make her feel whole again. Ava closed her eyes, a single tear trailing down her cheek, a crystalline drop of longing and regret.

In the stillness of the empty theater, Ava whispered a silent prayer, a plea to the universe, to fate itself. "Jamie," she breathed, her voice a trembling thread of hope, "I miss you."

As if summoned by her whispered plea, a familiar silhouette emerged from the shadows, a figure Ava would recognize anywhere. Jamie stood at the far end of the lobby, her hazel eyes locked on Ava, a mixture of longing and uncertainty etched across her face.

Ava's heart skipped a beat, her breath catching in her throat as she drank in the sight of the woman she had never truly forgotten. Jamie looked just as she remembered, her curly brown hair framing her face, her casual yet elegant attire hinting at the effortless beauty that had always taken Ava's breath away.

For a moment, they simply stared at each other, a silent conversation passing between them, a thousand unspoken words hanging in the air. The years melted away, and Ava found herself transported back to a time when their love had been the center of their universe, a force that had seemed unbreakable.

Ava's feet moved of their own accord, carrying her towards Jamie, drawn by an invisible thread that had never truly been severed. As she drew closer, she could see the flecks of gold in Jamie's eyes, the faint freckles that dusted her nose, the way her lips parted slightly, as if on the verge of speaking.

"Jamie," Ava breathed, her voice barely above a whisper, "I can't believe you're here."

Jamie's lips curved into a small, hesitant smile, a flicker of warmth in her eyes. "I couldn't miss your big night, Ava. Your play... it was incredible."

Ava's heart swelled with a mixture of pride and gratitude, the knowledge that Jamie had witnessed her triumph, had been there to share in her success. "Thank you," she murmured, her hand instinctively reaching out, fingers brushing against Jamie's arm, a fleeting touch that sent shivers down her spine.

The contact seemed to break the spell, and Jamie's gaze dropped to the floor, a faint blush coloring her cheeks. Ava's mind raced, a thousand questions bubbling to the surface, a desperate need to know everything about Jamie's life, to bridge the gap that time and circumstance had created between them.

"Jamie," Ava began, her voice trembling slightly, "I know it's been so long, but... can we talk? There's so much I want to say, so much I need to know."

Jamie's eyes met Ava's once more, a flicker of hesitation, of fear, dancing in their depths. But beneath it all, Ava could see the same longing, the same desire for connection, for closure, that burned within her own heart.

"Yes," Jamie whispered, her voice a gentle caress, "I think we should talk, Ava. There's so much left unsaid between us."

Ava nodded, her heart racing, her palms damp with anticipation. She gestured towards the theater doors, a silent invitation to step outside, to find a quiet place where they could finally unravel the tangled threads of their past.

As they walked side by side, their shoulders brushing, Ava felt a flicker of hope, a tiny flame that had never truly been extinguished. Perhaps, in the glow of the city lights, in the stillness of the night, they could find a way to heal, to forgive, to rediscover the love that had once been the very essence of their existence.

As they stepped into the cool night air, the bustling sounds of the theater lobby fading behind them, Ava led Jamie to a secluded bench nestled beneath the gentle glow of a streetlamp. The soft light cast a warm, intimate ambiance, as if the world had narrowed down to just the two of them, cocooned in a bubble of shared history and unspoken emotions.

Ava sat down, her fingers nervously tracing the worn wooden slats of the bench, as Jamie settled beside her, leaving a small but palpable space between them. The silence stretched, heavy with the weight of years, until Ava finally found her voice.

The things they each wanted to say to the other remained unspoken. Each afraid of experiencing the pain of rejection.

"I've missed you, Jamie," she longed to whisper, her words a gentle confession. *"Not a day has gone by that I haven't thought about you, about us, about what we had."*

Jamie's her eyes glistening with unshed tears. *"I've*

missed you, Ava. More than I ever thought possible," She longed to say.

Ava's heart swelled, a bittersweet ache blossoming in her chest. She longed to reach out, to take Jamie's hand in her own, to feel the familiar warmth of her skin, but she hesitated, unsure if the gesture would be welcomed.

"I know I hurt you, Jamie," Ava longed to express the weight of her regret. "I was so focused on my career, on proving myself to the world, that I lost sight of what truly mattered. I lost sight of you, of us."

Jamie's hazel eyes glazed over, aching to tell Ava, "We both made mistakes, Ava. We were young, and we had so much to learn about love, about life. I don't blame you for following your dreams."

Ava felt a tear slip down her cheek, the cool night air kissing her skin as she let out a shaky breath, thinking, "I should have fought for us, Jamie. I should have found a way to balance my passions, to make room for you in my life. I was so afraid of losing myself that I ended up losing the one person who truly saw me, who loved me for all that I was."

Jamie reached out then, her fingers gently brushing away Ava's tears, the tender touch sending a shiver down Ava's spine. She longed to say, "I never stopped loving you, Ava. Even when the pain was unbearable, even when I tried to move on, a part of my heart always belonged to you."

Ava leaned into Jamie's touch, her eyes fluttering closed as she savored the warmth of her skin, the familiar scent of her perfume. In that moment, the years melted away, and they were once again two young women, their hearts filled with the promise of forever.

"Do you think..." Ava imagined, her voice a fragile whisper, *"do you think we could try again? Could we find a way to forgive each other, to start anew?"*

Jamie's eyes searched Ava's, a flicker of hope dancing in their depths. *"I don't know what the future holds, Ava. But I do know that I'm tired of living in the past, of denying myself the chance to love, to be loved. If you're willing to try, to take things slow and see where this path leads us, then I'm here. I'm ready."*

Finally, Ave trusted herself to speak. A smile breaking through her tears, she nodded, her hand finding Jamie's and intertwining their fingers. "Jamie, can we get to know each other again."

Jamie nodded. "One step at a time."

As they sat there, their hands clasped, their hearts beating in sync, a physical manifestation of the emotional connection that had been rekindled. The distant sounds of the city—the hum of traffic, the occasional siren, the laughter of passersby—seemed muted, as if the world had faded into the background, leaving only the two of them in this moment.

Jamie turned to face Ava, her hazel eyes glimmering with a mix of anticipation and trepidation. "I guess this is where we say goodnight—for now," she murmured, her voice soft, almost hesitant.

Ava's heart fluttered, a bittersweet ache blooming in her chest.

"Let's exchange numbers," she suggested, her thumb tracing gentle circles on the back of Jamie's hand. "I don't want to lose touch with you again."

Jamie nodded, a small smile tugging at the corners of her lips as she reached into her purse and pulled out her phone. They exchanged devices, their fingers brushing against each other's skin as they typed in their contact information, a subtle reminder of the intimacy they had once shared.

As Ava saved her number in Jamie's phone, she paused, her gaze lingering on the screen. The weight of the past, of the unspoken words and unresolved emotions, pressed against her chest, threatening to steal her breath. But she pushed through, her fingers typing out a simple message: "To new beginnings."

Jamie's phone buzzed in Ava's hand, and she glanced down to see a reply: "To second chances."

Their eyes met, a silent acknowledgment of the journey that lay ahead, of the challenges they would face and the love they would fight for. Ava stepped closer, her free hand reaching up to tuck a stray curl behind Jamie's ear, her fingertips grazing the soft skin of her cheek.

"Goodnight, Jamie," Ava whispered, her voice thick with emotion. "I'll call you tomorrow."

Jamie leaned into Ava's touch, her eyes fluttering closed for a brief moment. "Look at me," Jamie commanded softly, gazing deep into Ava's eyes with a smoldering intensity that made her feel weak in the knees. Reluctantly but still complying, Ava met Jamie's gaze once more. The heat in those eyes made her feel like she was melting from the inside out.

Without further prompting, Jamie leaned in to capture Ava's lips. Their tongues danced together as one hand slid up underneath Ava's dress and pushed it high around her waist while the other teased between her legs to discover the damp fabric of her panties. Every touch sent a jolt of pleasure straight to her core and every moan from Jamie sent electricity surging through their connection.

It was as if no time had passed since their last encounter years ago as if they'd never been apart at all.

Ava's hands found their way into Jamie's hair, tangling in her soft locks as she pulled her closer still. She couldn't get enough of this - couldn't get enough of her. The fire between them burned hotter than ever before, only fueled by the years they had spent apart from one another. All thoughts of propriety and the world around them melted away as they continued their heated dance against the cool metal of a car door.

Jamie's fingers slid lower, delving beneath the fabric of Ava's panties to find the slick heat that awaited her. Ava gasped at the intimate touch, her back arching off the car as Jamie began to explore her folds with practiced ease – one finger, then two, stroking and teasing until Ava was on the edge of climax in record time. "J-Jamie," she panted out between ragged breaths, "I... I can't...not here."

Jamie didn't respond with words but instead picked up the pace, curling her fingers inside of Ava just so, hips grinding against hers once more as if to say 'I know.' Together they fell over the edge into oblivion, two bodies indivisible for those few brief moments where nothing else mattered but each other and the pleasure swirling between them both.

As their breathing finally began to slow and reality seeped back in, Jamie pulled away slightly, leaving a trail of kisses down Ava's neck until she reached her earlobe again. "I've missed you," she whispered before gently biting the tender skin just below her ear, sending shivers down Ava's spine once more. "I want you, Ava. Tonight. Tomorrow night. Every night after that..."

With a final squeeze of their hands, they parted ways, their hearts filled with a bittersweet mix of longing and hope. As Ava walked away, the click of her heels against the pavement echoing in the night, she couldn't help but glance back over her shoulder.

Jamie stood beneath the glow of the streetlamp, her silhouette cast in a soft, golden light. She raised her hand in a small wave, a gesture that spoke volumes, a promise of the love that had never truly died.

Ava turned back, her steps lighter, her heart fuller. The road ahead was uncertain, but one thing was clear: she and Jamie had been given a second chance, a opportunity to heal, to love, to rediscover the magic that had once brought them together.

Two

THEY MET AGAIN, both guests at a mutual friends wedding at the Windemere Estate. The soft glow of fairy lights danced across Ava's skin as she stepped into the enchanted garden, her emerald green dress swishing gently around her ankles. The scent of jasmine and rose mingled in the air, a heady perfume that made her pulse quicken. She inhaled deeply, trying to calm the flutter of nerves in her stomach.

This is it, she thought, scanning the crowd of elegantly dressed guests. *The moment I've both dreaded and longed for.*

Her eyes roamed over the sea of faces, searching for the one that still haunted her dreams. And then, as if pulled by an invisible thread, her gaze locked with a pair of familiar hazel eyes across the garden.

Jamie.

Ava's breath caught in her throat. Jamie looked stunning in a sleek navy dress that hugged her curves, her chestnut hair swept up to reveal the graceful line of her neck. Even from a distance, Ava could feel the electricity crackling between them, a current of unspoken history and unresolved desire.

After all these years, she still takes my breath away, Ava marveled silently, her heart pounding against her ribcage. Memories flooded unbidden into her mind—stolen kisses, hushed promises, the searing pain of goodbye. She swallowed hard, pushing them back into the recesses of her heart.

Jamie's eyes widened slightly, a flicker of surprise and something else—longing, perhaps?—passing over her features. Her lips curved into a tentative smile, a silent acknowledgement of the connection that still tethered them together.

Ava found herself smiling back, a bittersweet ache blooming in her chest. She wanted to rush to her, to bridge the distance that time and circumstance had wedged between them. But uncertainty held her back, the fear of reopening old wounds, of facing the ghosts of their shared past.

Not yet, she told herself, tearing her gaze away reluctantly. *There will be time to talk, to untangle the knots we left behind.*

She lost herself in the crowd, the air suddenly too thick to breathe. The fairy lights blurred, casting a dreamlike haze over the garden. But even as she moved away, Ava could feel the weight of Jamie's eyes on her back, a silent promise of the conversation to come.

Ava took a deep breath, the floral scent of the garden mingling with the faint aroma of Jamie's perfume that lingered in her memory. Mustering every ounce of courage, she turned and began to weave through the crowd, her steps measured yet determined. The chatter of the guests faded into a distant hum as her focus narrowed on the woman who had once held her heart.

Navigating around groups of chatting guests, Ava felt as if she were moving through a dream, each step bringing her closer to a moment she had both longed for and dreaded. The air seemed to shimmer with anticipation, the very atoms charged with the unspoken emotions that swirled between them.

As she approached, Jamie's eyes widened in surprise, a myriad of emotions flickering across her face like shadows cast by a candle's flame. A soft smile tugged at the corners of her lips, a gesture that sent Ava's heart stuttering in her chest.

"Ava," Jamie breathed, her voice a mixture of warmth and restraint.

Ava drank in the sight of Jamie, noticing the faint lines

around her eyes that spoke of laughter and the passage of time. "You look beautiful, as always."

Jamie ducked her head, a faint blush coloring her cheeks. "Thank you. You're quite stunning yourself."

They stood there for a moment, the air between them thick with unspoken words and memories that threatened to spill forth. Ava's fingers itched to reach out, to trace the curve of Jamie's cheek, to feel the warmth of her skin beneath her fingertips.

What are we doing? Ava wondered, her heart racing. *Can we really pick up where we left off, after all this time?*

But even as the doubts swirled in her mind, Ava knew that she couldn't walk away, not again. The magnetic pull that had always existed between them was still there, stronger than ever, drawing her in like a moth to a flame.

"I've missed you," Ava whispered, the words slipping out before she could stop them. "More than you know."

Jamie's eyes glistened with unshed tears, a reflection of the emotions that churned within Ava's own heart. "I've missed you too, Ava. Every single day."

The world around them seemed to fade away, the wedding guests becoming nothing more than blurred shapes in the periphery of their vision. In that moment, it was just the two of them, lost in a bubble of their own making, where the past and present collided in a bitter-sweet dance of longing and possibility.

Ava's gaze darted to the bustling wedding reception,

the laughter and chatter of the guests a stark contrast to the tension that hung between them. She turned back to Jamie, her voice low and tinged with a hint of desperation. "Can we go somewhere quieter? Somewhere we can talk, just the two of us?"

Jamie hesitated for a moment, her eyes searching Ava's face as if trying to decipher the unspoken emotions that lay beneath the surface. Then, with a small nod, she gestured towards a secluded corner of the garden, where the twinkling fairy lights gave way to the soft glow of the moon.

They made their way through the garden, the gravel path crunching beneath their feet, the sound of the wedding reception fading into the background. The air was heavy with the scent of blooming roses and honey-suckle, a heady perfume that seemed to wrap around them like a delicate cocoon.

As they reached the secluded corner, Ava's breath caught in her throat. A weathered wooden bench sat beneath a canopy of trees, their leaves rustling gently in the breeze. It was as if the world had crafted this very spot for them, a sanctuary where they could finally confront the ghosts of their past.

They settled onto the bench, their bodies angled towards each other, knees almost touching. Ava's heart thrummed in her chest, a wild bird seeking escape from its cage. She could feel the heat of Jamie's skin, so close and yet so far, a tantalizing reminder of the intimacy they had once shared.

Jamie's eyes, those hazel depths that had once been Ava's anchor, now held a storm of emotions. Fear, longing, and a flicker of hope danced behind her guarded expression, a silent plea for Ava to bridge the chasm that had grown between them.

Ava's fingers twitched, aching to reach out and trace the delicate line of Jamie's jaw, to feel the softness of her skin beneath her touch. But she held back, the weight of their history pressing down upon her like a physical force.

Where do we go from here? Ava wondered, her mind spinning with a thousand possibilities. *Can we find our way back to each other, or has too much time passed, too many wounds left unhealed?*

The air crackled with tension, the unspoken words hanging between them like a tangible presence. Ava could feel the heat of Jamie's gaze, the intensity of it sending shivers down her spine. She knew that they were balancing on a knife's edge, teetering between the past and the present, between the love they had once shared and the uncertainty of what lay ahead.

"Jamie, I..." Ava began, her voice barely above a whisper. But the words stuck in her throat, the enormity of all that needed to be said threatening to overwhelm her.

Jamie's hand twitched, as if fighting the urge to reach

out and touch Ava. Her voice was soft, almost breathless. "I know, Ava. I know."

And in that moment, as the moon cast its gentle light upon them and the breeze carried the sweet scent of promise, Ava knew that they had taken the first step towards healing, towards finding their way back to each other. The road ahead would be long and winding, but with Jamie by her side, she was ready to face whatever lay in store.

Ava's heart fluttered in her chest as she mustered the courage to ask the question that had been burning inside her for years. "What have you been doing since we last saw each other, Jamie? How has life treated you?"

Jamie's hazel eyes softened, a wistful smile playing on her lips. "I've been teaching, Ava. High school English. It's been my passion, my salvation in many ways." Her voice grew tender, almost reverent. "There's something magical about guiding young minds, helping them discover the power of literature, the beauty of words."

Ava leaned closer, drawn in by the warmth and sincerity in Jamie's voice. She could picture Jamie in the classroom, her gentle presence commanding attention, her love for the written word shining through in every lesson.

"I've always admired your way with words, Jamie," Ava murmured, her fingers itching to reach out and trace the delicate lines of Jamie's face. "The way you could make even the most complex ideas come alive, the way you could inspire others to see the world through a different lens."

Jamie ducked her head, a faint blush coloring her cheeks. "It's been a privilege, Ava. To be able to make a difference in my students' lives, to help them find their own voices and passions."

The air between them hummed with a quiet intensity, the weight of unspoken emotions pressing against their chests. Ava's heart raced as she allowed herself to truly see Jamie, to appreciate the woman she had become in the years they had been apart.

She's even more beautiful than I remembered, Ava thought, her gaze tracing the gentle curve of Jamie's jaw, the way her curls framed her face like a halo. *How could I have ever let her go?*

"And what about you, Ava?" Jamie asked softly, her eyes searching Ava's face. "How has the world of theater been treating you?"

Ava's lips quirked into a wry smile. "It's been a roller-coaster, Jamie. The highs are incredible, but the lows..." She trailed off, shaking her head. "Sometimes I wonder if it's all worth it, if the sacrifices I've made have been too great."

Jamie's hand twitched, as if fighting the urge to reach out and offer comfort. "You've always had a gift, Ava. A way of capturing the human experience, of making people feel seen and understood."

Ava's breath caught in her throat, the sincerity in Jamie's words piercing through the layers of doubt and insecurity that had built up over the years. In that moment, under the gentle glow of the moonlight, Ava felt a flicker of hope reignite in her chest.

Maybe it's not too late, she thought, her heart swelling with a bittersweet longing. *Maybe we can find our way back to each other, back to the love we once shared.*

The breeze picked up, rustling the leaves overhead and carrying with it the faint strains of music from the distant wedding reception. Ava and Jamie sat in silence, their bodies angled towards each other, their eyes locked in a dance of unspoken emotions.

And as the night wore on, the stars twinkling above them like a thousand possibilities, Ava knew that this was only the beginning. The beginning of a journey towards healing, towards forgiveness, towards a future that held the promise of a love rekindled and a bond unbroken.

Ava took a deep breath, summoning the courage that had long lain dormant within her. The air around them seemed to still, as if the very universe was holding its breath in anticipation of her next words.

"Jamie," she whispered, her voice trembling with the weight of years of unspoken regrets. "I've never stopped thinking about you, about what we had. About what we could have been."

Jamie's eyes widened, a flicker of surprise and something deeper, something achingly familiar, dancing within their hazel depths. Her lips parted slightly, as if to speak, but Ava pressed on, determined to lay her heart bare.

"I know I hurt you, all those years ago. I was young and foolish, too caught up in my own dreams to see what truly mattered. But not a day has gone by that I haven't regretted letting you go."

Ava's hand inched closer to Jamie's, their fingers mere centimeters apart, the space between them charged with a yearning that transcended time and distance.

Jamie's gaze softened, a hint of moisture glistening at the corners of her eyes. "Ava," she breathed, her voice barely above a whisper. "I... I never stopped thinking about you, either. But so much time has passed. We've both changed. How can we be sure...?"

Ava's fingers brushed against Jamie's, a feather-light touch that sent sparks racing up her arm. "We can't be sure of anything," she murmured, her eyes locked with Jamie's. "But what I do know is that the love I felt for you, the love I still feel... it's real. And it's worth fighting for."

The air between them crackled with tension, with the unspoken desires and the weight of years of longing. Jamie's hand trembled beneath Ava's, a silent acknowledgment of the emotions that swirled between them.

"I'm scared, Ava," Jamie whispered, her voice raw with vulnerability. "Scared of opening myself up again, of risking my heart. But..."

Ava leaned closer, her face mere inches from Jamie's, their breaths mingling in the scant space between them. "But?" she prompted, her heart thundering in her chest.

Jamie's eyes fluttered closed, a single tear escaping down her cheek. "But I'm even more scared of letting you go again, of living a life without you in it."

And with those words, the last of the walls between them crumbled, giving way to a tidal wave of emotion that had been held at bay for far too long. Ava's lips found Jamie's, a soft, tentative kiss that slowly deepened, their mouths moving in a dance of rediscovery and reignited passion.

The world around them faded away, the distant laughter and music from the wedding reception nothing more than a faint echo in the background. In that moment, beneath the canopy of stars and the gentle rustling of leaves, Ava and Jamie found each other again, their hearts intertwining in a silent promise of a future filled with love, healing, and the courage to face whatever lay ahead, together.

As their kiss subsided, they remained entwined in each

other's arms, their foreheads pressed together, their breathing still ragged. A gentle breeze caressed their skin, carrying with it the fragrance of jasmine, the sweet scent a symbol of their newfound chance at love.

"I don't ever want to let you go again," Ava murmured, her voice husky with emotion.

Jamie smiled, her eyes shining with unshed tears. "Neither do I."

Together, they walked back to the reception, their fingers laced together, their steps lighter, their hearts lighter still, buoyed by the knowledge that sometimes, love really does find a way to write the most beautiful of second acts.

And as the evening drew to a close, as the last notes of the string quartet faded into the night, Ava and Jamie found themselves standing at the edge of a new beginning, a promise of forever dawning like the light of a thousand stars in their eyes.

They walked together to the carpark, lingering in the shadow beneath curb-side trees long after everyone else had left. Their pasts no longer shadows, but rather pages in a story that had led them to this moment, to this love, they embraced the uncertainty of the future with hope and joy, their hearts finally free to dance the dance of true and lasting love.

Away from prying eyes. As their lips connected, Ava's eyes fluttered open, her gaze locking with Jamie's. In the depths of those hazel eyes, she saw a reflection of her own longing, a mirror of the years spent yearning for the touch of the woman she had never truly forgotten. Jamie's hand reached up, her fingers brushing gently against Ava's cheek, tracing the contours of her face as if committing every detail to memory.

"I've missed you," Jamie breathed, her voice barely above a whisper. "Every day, every moment, I've carried you with me."

Ava leaned into Jamie's touch, her skin tingling beneath the warmth of her fingertips. "I never stopped loving you," she confessed, the words tumbling from her lips like a secret finally set free. "Even when I tried to convince myself otherwise, my heart always belonged to you."

Jamie's eyes glistened with unshed tears, a soft smile tugging at the corners of her mouth.

Ava and Jamie pulled apart, their faces flushed with a mix of desire and frustration. The spell that had enveloped them moments before dissipated, replaced by the harsh reality of the world around them.

Ava's heart raced, her mind reeling from the intensity of the emotions that had surged through her. She couldn't help but feel a pang of disappointment, a longing for the moment that had been so abruptly interrupted.

Jamie reached out, her hand finding Ava's, their fingers intertwining in a silent gesture of understanding.

"We should probably head back," she said softly, her voice tinged with reluctance. "But this isn't over, Ava. We have so much more to say, so much more to explore."

Ava nodded, a flicker of hope igniting in her chest. "You're right," she agreed, squeezing Jamie's hand. "This is just the beginning."

Ava's mind swirled with a kaleidoscope of emotions. The taste of Jamie's lips lingered on her own, a tantalizing reminder of the love they had rediscovered. And though the path ahead was uncertain, one thing was clear: she would never let Jamie slip away again.

"I don't want to let this moment slip away," Ava whispered, her voice barely audible above the distant hum of the wedding reception. "Not again."

Jamie's hazel eyes softened, a flicker of hope dancing within their depths. "Then let's not," she replied, her fingers gently brushing against Ava's arm, sending a shiver down her spine. "Meet me tomorrow, at the old willow tree by the river. The one where we used to..."

"I remember," Ava breathed, her heart skipping a beat at the memory of stolen kisses and whispered promises beneath the tree's graceful branches.

Ava's mind raced with the possibilities of what tomorrow might bring. "Tomorrow," she agreed, her voice trembling slightly. "We'll finally have a chance to..."

"To talk," Jamie finished, a hint of a smile tugging at

the corners of her lips. "To finally say everything we've been holding back."

Ava nodded.

But as she looked into Jamie's eyes, Ava saw a reflection of her own longing, a shared desire to rekindle the love they had once known. As they reluctantly parted ways, Ava's thoughts were consumed by the promise of tomorrow, of the chance to finally lay bare the secrets of her heart.

Three

AS THE NIGHT SKY DARKENED, Ava and Jamie found themselves alone in the dimly lit parking lot, their heart racing with anticipation. The other guests had left. The familiar scent of oil and pavement filled their nostrils, mingling with the cool autumn breeze that rustled through the trees nearby. Their thoughts were consumed by the kiss they'd shared earlier, the electricity that had surged between them.

Ava couldn't believe Jamie had felt the same way all these years. It was like a dream come true - or rather, a long-forgotten memory resurfacing to haunt her in the best possible way.

Ava took a deep breath and followed Jamie towards Jamie's car. Her heart thumped erratically in her chest as she approached the vehicle, hidden in the shadows of the lot where only a sliver of moonlight could reach them. She couldn't help but wonder what would happen next. Would they pick up where they left off earlier? Or would this be another false start?

She heard the click of a car door opening behind her and turned around to see Jamie in the darkness urging her to get in.

Jamie's eyes met Ava's for a moment before drifting down to admire her body, taking in every curve and line. Ava felt exposed under this gaze, yet strangely empowered as well. The air crackled between them, electric once more as Jamie approached slowly, her heels clicking against the pavement.

"Here we are," Jamie purred, voice low and seductive.

Jamie's hands trailed up Ava's thigh, ghosts of touches from their past lingering in the air. Ava shivered as her skin tingled under Jamie's fingertips. She could feel the heat emanating from within her body, her core pulsating with need. Jamie backed her against the car, their hips grinding together in a primal dance that sent waves of pleasure coursing through them both. Her lips parted in invitation, and without hesitation, Ava felt Jamie's tongue dart out to taste hers once more. The kiss was fierce, demanding, possessive - everything she had always wanted and more.

Breaking away for air, Jamie looked deep into Ava's eyes with a smoldering gaze that promised things to come. "I've missed this," she whispered hoarsely before leaning down to nibble on her earlobe, sending shockwaves of desire straight to Ava's core. "You have no idea how long I've dreamt of doing this again." Her breath fanned across Ava's neck as she trailed kisses down towards her collarbone, while one hand slid up underneath her dress to tease dangerously close to where they were pressed together.

Ava gasped at the contact but didn't pull away as Jamie reached higher still until fingertips brushed against her slick folds through the cotton of her panties. She moaned into the night air as Jamie began to stroke gently; each touch making her wetter than before, each sound of pleasure echoing in the dark stillness around them like a seductive melody. It felt so good - too good - yet she couldn't help but wonder if this was

Jamie's hands slid up Ava's thigh, pushing her dress further up as her lips trailed fire on Ava's neck. Ava gasped, arching into the touch. "You taste so fucking good," Jamie purred against her skin, nipping lightly as she spoke. "And you feel even better." She pulled back to look down at Ava, their eyes locking together in a heated gaze as her thumb teased across the sensitive nub between her legs through the thin material of her panties. Ava gasped, biting her lip and looking away, trying to resist the desire pulsing through her body. "Look at me," Jamie commanded softly, and Ava did—reluctantly but still complying. Her eyes met Jamie's once more. The heat in them made Ava feel weak in the knees.

Jamie grinned wickedly before leaning in to take another kiss, this one even hotter than before. Her tongue danced around Ava's lips before slipping inside, teasing and tasting while her hips ground against hers once more. Ava groaned into the kiss, unable to resist as Jamie's hands slid underneath her dress and pushed aside the lace of her panties. Fingers slid between folds slick with anticipation and desire, parting them for intrusion that seemed inevitable now.

"You know you want this," Jamie breathed against Ava's ear, teeth grazing her lobe as she continued to explore every inch of exposed skin.

Ava shivered as her skin tingled under Jamie's fingertips. She could feel the heat emanating from within her body, her core pulsating with need. Jamie backed her against the car, their hips grinding together in a primal dance that sent waves of pleasure coursing through them both. Her lips parted in invitation, and without hesitation, Ava felt Jamie's tongue dart out to taste hers once more. The kiss was fierce, demanding, possessive - everything she had always wanted and more.

Breaking away for air, Jamie looked deep into Ava's eyes with a smoldering gaze that promised things to come. "I've missed this," she whispered hoarsely before leaning down to nibble on her earlobe, sending shockwaves of desire straight to Ava's core. "You have no idea how long I've dreamt of doing this again." Her breath fanned across Ava's neck as she trailed kisses down towards her collarbone, while one hand slid up underneath her dress, pushing it higher until it bunched around her waist. The other hand slid up her thigh, pressing against her slick folds beneath the thin material of her panties. Ava gasped at the contact but didn't pull away as Jamie's fingers teased dangerously close to where they were pressed together. Each touch made her wetter than before; each sound of pleasure echoing in the dark stillness around them like a seductive melody only fueled the flame inside of her. "Look at me," Jamie commanded softly; Ava did - complying with the command. Their eyes locked once more in a heated gaze that made Ava weak at

Ava gasped as Jamie's lips trailed lower, kissing her neck, nipping lightly with her teeth. She ground her hips against Jamie's, desperate for more contact, feeling the heat between her legs build with every passing moment. Jamie's breath was hot against her skin, each inhalation and exhalation sending shivers down Ava's spine. Her fingers played beneath the lace of Ava's panties, slowly pulling them aside to reveal the wetness that had pooled there.

"You taste so fucking good," Jamie purred into Ava's ear, her voice low and husky. "And you feel even better." Her thumb rubbed teasingly against Ava's clit through the thin material of her panties, sending shockwaves of pleasure coursing through every inch of her body. Despite herself, Ava arched into the touch, moaning softly.

Jamie's touch against Ava's skin was driving her wild with desire. As Jamie's fingers plunged deeper into her folds, she couldn't help but gasp out loud, her hips bucking against the hard surface of the car in a desperate search for more contact. The taste of her lover on her lips made her dizzy with need, and she couldn't resist any longer when those fingers found their way to her clit. Arching into the touch, Ava moaned softly as Jamie began to tease and taunt her, circling and pressing just hard enough to drive her mad. She could feel herself becoming wetter by the second as Jamie pushed her limits further.

"You like this, don't you?" Jamie whispered against Ava's earlobe, nipping it gently between her teeth before soothing it with gentle kisses. Her other hand slid up underneath Ava's dress once more, this time cupping one perfect breast through her lace bra as she pinched and rolled the nipple between thumb and forefinger. Jamie pulled back slightly to look into Ava's eyes again, seeing the desire burning bright in them despite her attempts to deny it. "Admit it," she said huskily. "You want me."

Ava shook her head no even as she groaned yes inside. The feeling of being taken like this was like nothing else, but she knew they couldn't stop here. They were in public; someone could see them at any moment. Yet still, she couldn't deny the pull of Jamie's touch or the way it made every nerve ending in her body tingle with anticipation. "I... I shouldn't," she managed to whisper.

Jamie knelt at Ava's feet, tenderly removing her panties with trembling hands. Her lips brushed against Ava's clit, sending shivers of pleasure through her body. Slowly, she explored every inch of Ava's sex, teasing and tasting until they were both breathless with desire.

As Jamie's tongue flicked against her clit, Ava couldn't hold back anymore. With a gasp, she bucked her hips and grabbed onto Jamie's hair, pulling her closer as the pleasure built within her. Every touch of Jamie's lips and fingers was like fire on her skin, driving her closer to the edge with every passing second.

"Please," she moaned, her voice filled with need. "I need you."

Jamie didn't respond with words, instead she slid two fingers inside of Ava and curled them just right to hit that spot that made Ava see stars. She continued to suck and lick at Ava's clit, sending her to heights of pleasure she had never experienced before. Waves of ecstasy washed over Ava as Jamie expertly worked her body, bringing her closer and closer to the brink.

Just when Ava thought she couldn't take any more, Jamie added a third finger and sucked harder on her clit. The combination was too much for Ava to handle and with a loud cry, she climaxed hard against Jamie's mouth. Her entire body shook with the force of it as Jamie continued to work through her orgasm until finally she collapsed back against the car seat.

Jamie pulled back slowly, a satisfied smirk on her face as she licked her lips clean of Ava's juices. She stood, leaning in for a passionate kiss, tasting herself on Jamie's lips.

After catching their breaths and recovering from their intense encounter, they straightened themselves out and fixed their appearance. They were both still flushed and slightly disheveled, but they didn't care.

"Come home with me?" Jamie asked.

"I can't." Ava shook her head. "I have an early appointment." She giggled. "I need to clear my head. I 'm going to have to work to thinking straight again—after that."

"Then, goodbye —for now, Ava."

"Good bye, Jamie."

Four

THE AROMA of freshly brewed coffee enveloped Ava as she stepped into Toby's living room, a welcoming embrace in the midst of her inner turmoil. She sank into the plush cushions of the couch, its softness a fleeting comfort against the weight of her thoughts. Toby looked up from his book, setting it aside with a gentle thud. His warm hazel eyes met hers, a flicker of concern dancing within their depths.

"Ava," he said softly, his voice a soothing balm to her frayed nerves. "What's on your mind?"

She fidgeted with the hem of her sweater, the fabric twisting between her restless fingers. The words caught in her throat, tangled in a web of uncertainty and fear. How could she voice the tempest raging within her heart? The longing, the ache, the desperate desire to love and be loved in return?

Toby leaned forward, his elbows resting on his knees as he studied her face. "You know you can talk to me about anything, right?"

Ava nodded, swallowing hard. She knew Toby would understand, would offer the comfort and guidance she so desperately needed. And yet, the fear of judgment, of rejection, lingered like a shadow at the edges of her mind.

She took a deep breath, the scent of coffee mingling with the faint traces of Toby's cologne - a familiar, grounding aroma. "I... I've been thinking about love," she began, her voice barely above a whisper. "About taking risks and following my heart, even when it terrifies me."

Toby's expression softened, a knowing glint in his eyes. He reached out, his hand resting gently on her shoulder.

"Love is always a risk," he said, his voice low and soothing. "But it's a risk worth taking, Ava. You deserve happiness, and sometimes that means stepping out of your comfort zone."

Ava's eyes flickered to the window, where the afternoon sun cast dappled shadows across the hardwood floor.

"I'm scared, Toby," she admitted, her voice trembling. "Scared of getting hurt, of being judged, of losing myself in the process."

Toby squeezed her shoulder gently, his touch a lifeline in the tumultuous sea of her emotions. "I know it's scary, but you're stronger than you give yourself credit for. You've faced challenges before and emerged even more resilient. Trust yourself, Ava. Trust your heart."

As Ava met Toby's gaze, she saw the unwavering love and support that had always been there, a constant lighthouse guiding her through the storms of life.

Perhaps Toby was right. Perhaps it was time to take a leap of faith, to embrace the love that called to her, no matter how daunting the journey ahead might be. With her brother by her side, Ava felt a renewed sense of strength coursing through her veins.

She took a sip of the coffee Toby had brewed, its rich flavor warming her from within. The scent, the taste, the gentle hum of the room - all of it seemed to whisper promises of a brighter future, one where love could conquer fear and happiness could be found in the most unexpected places.

Ava's fingers curled around the warm ceramic mug, the heat seeping into her skin as she drew in a steadying breath. The rich aroma of coffee mingled with the faint scent of aged paper and well-worn leather, a comforting blend that seemed to envelope her in Toby's familiar presence. She looked up at her brother, her voice wavering slightly as she began to speak.

"I never thought I'd see her again, Toby. After all these

years, I'd convinced myself that I'd moved on, that Jamie was just a distant memory." Ava's gaze drifted to the window, the soft afternoon light filtering through the sheer curtains. "But then, there she was, standing right in front of me, and it was like no time had passed at all."

Toby leaned forward, his elbows resting on his knees as he listened intently. "What did you feel when you saw her, Ava?" His voice was gentle, coaxing her to delve deeper into the emotions that swirled within her.

"It was like a tidal wave crashing over me," Ava admitted, her fingers tightening around the mug. "All the love, the heartache, the unresolved feelings - they came rushing back in an instant. I thought I'd buried them deep enough, but seeing Jamie again... it made me realize that they'd never truly gone away."

"I'm scared, Toby. Scared of what people will think, of the whispers and the judgment. But more than that, I'm terrified of getting hurt again. Of opening myself up to love, only to have it slip through my fingers once more."

Toby nodded slowly, his expression one of understanding. "It's natural to feel that way, Ava. Love is a risk, and it takes courage to embrace it, especially when you've been hurt before." He reached out, his hand covering hers in a gesture of support. "But think about what you felt when you saw Jamie again. That spark, that connection - it's rare and precious. Don't let fear rob you of the chance to explore it."

Ava's heart raced at the thought, a mixture of exhilaration and trepidation coursing through her veins. She knew Toby was right, that the love she felt for Jamie was worth fighting for.

"What if it doesn't work out?" she whispered, her voice barely audible above the gentle hum of the room. "What if I put my heart on the line, only to have it shattered once again?"

Toby squeezed her hand, his gaze filled with empathy and understanding. "That's a risk we all take when we choose to love, Ava. But think about the alternative - a life lived in the shadow of fear, never knowing the joy and fulfillment that true love can bring. Is that really what you want?"

Ava closed her eyes, images of Jamie flooding her mind.

She opened her eyes, a newfound determination shining within their depths. "No," she said firmly, her voice growing stronger with each word. "I don't want to live a life dictated by fear. I want to take a chance on love, on Jamie, no matter how scary it might be."

Toby smiled, pride and affection evident in his expression. He

Toby's hand rested on Ava's shoulder, a comforting weight that anchored her amidst the tempest of emotions swirling within. His voice, soft yet resolute, cut through the silence. "Your feelings, Ava, they're real.

They matter. You deserve happiness, more than anyone I know."

Ava's eyes glistened, tears threatening to spill over as she absorbed his words. She drew in a shaky breath, the scent of coffee mingling with the faint traces of Toby's cologne—a familiar combination that evoked memories of countless heart-to-heart conversations shared between siblings.

"But what if I'm just setting myself up for heartbreak again?" The words tumbled from her lips, raw and vulnerable. "I've been down this road before, Toby. I've taken risks, only to end up shattered and alone." Her voice cracked, a single tear escaping and trickling down her cheek.

Toby's fingers tightened on her shoulder, a gentle squeeze that conveyed his understanding. "I know, Ava. I know how much you've been through, how much you've had to pick yourself up and start anew. But you can't let the fear of the past dictate your future."

Ava's gaze drifted to the window, the soft afternoon light filtering through the sheer curtains.

What if I'm not strong enough? The thought echoed in her mind, a persistent whisper that had haunted her for far too long. *What if I'm just destined to repeat the same mistakes, to find myself once again nursing a broken heart?*

But even as the doubts threatened to consume her, Toby's presence remained steadfast. His hand moved from her shoulder to her back, rubbing soothing circles as she wept. In that moment, Ava realized that the strength she sought had been within her all along—a resilience forged through the fires of heartache and disappointment.

She opened her eyes, meeting Toby's gaze through a veil of tears. In the depths of his hazel eyes, she saw a reflection of her own soul—scared, yet hopeful; wounded, yet resilient. And in that shared understanding, she found the courage to take a step forward, to embrace the possibility of love, no matter how daunting the journey ahead might be.

Toby's voice, soft and reassuring, broke through the silence that had settled between them. "Ava, I know you're scared. I know the thought of opening your heart again feels like a risk you might not be ready to take. But let me tell you something I've learned over the years..."

He leaned back against the couch, his gaze drifting to the framed photographs on the mantelpiece—snapshots of a life well-lived, of love lost and found. "When I met Sarah, I was a mess. My heart had been broken so many times, I didn't think I had anything left to give. But she saw something in me, something I couldn't see myself. And despite all my fears, despite all the reasons I had to walk away... I took a chance."

Ava watched as a wistful smile played across Toby's lips, his eyes shining with the memory of a love that had changed his life. "It wasn't easy, Ava. There were times when I wanted to run, when I was convinced that I was making a mistake. But Sarah... she was patient. She was kind. And she showed me that love, real love, is worth fighting for."

He turned to face Ava once more, his expression earnest and sincere. "I know you're afraid of getting hurt again. I know the thought of putting your heart on the line feels like a gamble you might not win. But Ava, if there's one thing I've learned, it's that the greatest rewards in life come from the risks we're willing to take."

Ava felt the tension in her shoulders begin to ease, Toby's words washing over her like a soothing balm. She knew he was right—that the path to happiness was rarely a smooth one, that the most meaningful connections were often forged in the fires of uncertainty and doubt.

"I just... I don't know if I'm brave enough, Toby." Her voice was barely a whisper, the admission hanging heavy in the air between them. "What if I take this chance, and it all falls apart? What if I'm not..."

"Enough?" Toby finished, his tone gentle but firm. "Ava, you are more than enough. You always have been. And anyone who can't see that, who can't appreciate the incredible woman you are... they don't deserve you."

He reached out, taking her hand in his own, his touch a silent promise of support and understanding. "I know it's scary, Ava. I know the thought of letting someone in, of exposing your heart to the possibility of pain... it's terrifying. But I also know that you have a strength within you that is greater than any fear, any doubt."

"Thank you, Toby." Her voice was thick with emotion, the words inadequate to express the depth of her gratitude. "I don't know what I would do without you."

Toby smiled, the warmth of his expression chasing away the last of the shadows that had gathered in Ava's heart. "You'll never have to find out, sis. I'll always be here, no matter what. And I know, without a doubt, that you have the strength to face whatever comes your way. You just have to trust yourself, trust the love that's waiting for you on the other side of fear."

Ava drew in a deep breath, the scent of coffee and the familiar comfort of Toby's living room grounding her in the present moment. She closed her eyes for a heartbeat, allowing her brother's words to sink into her very bones, to fortify the fragile hope that had taken root within her.

"You're right, Toby. I've been running from my feelings for so long, afraid of what might happen if I let myself truly embrace them. But I can't keep living in fear, can't keep denying myself the chance at happiness."

Toby's smile widened, pride and affection shining in his hazel eyes. "That's my girl. I know it won't be easy, but I also know that you have the courage to face whatever challenges come your way. And you won't be facing them alone. I'll be right here, every step of the way."

Ava felt a smile tugging at her own lips, a sense of

lightness spreading through her chest as if a weight had been lifted from her heart. She stood up from the couch, her posture straight and her head held high, a woman ready to embrace the future that lay before her.

"I'm going to do it, Toby. I'm going to take a chance on love, on happiness. I'm going to trust my heart, even if it means risking everything."

Toby rose to his feet, pulling Ava into a tight embrace, his arms a fortress of love and support. "I'm so proud of you, Ava. And I know, without a shadow of a doubt, that you're making the right choice. Love is always worth the risk."

As Ava stepped back from the embrace, she felt a newfound sense of purpose thrumming through her veins, a fierce determination to seize the happiness that had eluded her for so long. She knew the road ahead wouldn't be easy, but with Toby by her side and the strength of her own heart to guide her, she was ready to face whatever challenges lay ahead.

For the first time in years, Ava allowed herself to believe in the possibility of a future filled with love and joy, a future where she could finally be true to herself and the desires of her heart. And as she strode towards the door, ready to take on the world, she knew that nothing could stand in the way of a woman determined to claim her destiny.

Five

～

THE BELL above the door chimed as Ava stepped into the cozy warmth of Lena's coffee shop, a welcome respite from the biting chill outside. The rich aroma of freshly ground espresso beans and the gentle hum of conversation enveloped her like a comforting embrace. Her emerald eyes scanned the room, searching for the familiar face that had been her anchor in times of inner turmoil.

Ava's heart thrummed against her ribcage, a mixture of anticipation and trepidation coursing through her veins. It had been too long since their last encounter, and the weight of unspoken words pressed heavily upon her chest. She wove her way through the labyrinth of tables and chairs, her steps hesitant yet determined, driven by an inexplicable force that pulled her toward the one person who seemed to understand the depths of her soul.

And there she was, nestled in a corner table, a beacon of serenity amidst the bustling café. Lena looked up from the worn pages of a book, her warm brown eyes lighting up with recognition and a tenderness that soothed Ava's frayed nerves. A gentle smile played upon Lena's lips, a silent invitation for Ava to join her in this intimate moment.

Ava's fingers trembled slightly as she smoothed the fabric of her tailored coat, a futile attempt to calm the tempest within. She stood before Lena, her voice caught in her throat, unsure of how to begin. The years stretched between them, a chasm filled with unspoken longing and the echoes of a love that had never quite faded.

"Ava, my dear," Lena's voice was a soothing balm, her tone laced with genuine affection. "It's so good to see you. Please, sit."

Ava sank into the chair opposite Lena, her body molding to the contours of the worn leather. She inhaled deeply, the scent of cinnamon and vanilla mingling with the earthy aroma of the café. It was a fragrance that had become synonymous with comfort, with the solace she sought in times of inner turmoil.

Lena reached across the table, her fingers brushing against Ava's hand in a gesture of understanding. The touch was electric, sending a shiver down Ava's spine and igniting a spark within her heart. It was a reminder of the connection they shared, a bond forged through shared experiences and the unspoken secrets that lingered between them.

"I'm so glad you came," Lena said softly, her eyes searching Ava's face, as if trying to decipher the tempest of emotions swirling beneath the surface. "I could sense that you needed to talk, to unburden yourself of the weight you carry."

Ava swallowed hard, her throat constricting with the intensity of her feelings. She had come here seeking guidance, seeking the comfort that only Lena could provide. Yet now, in the presence of the one person who understood her most intimately, the words seemed to evaporate, leaving her tongue-tied and vulnerable.

"Lena, I..." Ava began, her voice trembling with the rawness of her emotions. "I don't know where to begin. There's so much I need to say, so much I've been holding inside."

Lena's gaze softened, her eyes shimmering with a depth of empathy that threatened to unravel Ava's carefully constructed façade. "Take your time, my dear. I'm here to listen, to help you navigate the labyrinth of your heart. We have all the time in the world."

Ava nodded, taking a shaky breath as she allowed herself to sink into the comfort of Lena's presence. In this sacred space, surrounded by the warmth of the café and the understanding of a kindred spirit, she knew that she could finally confront the ghosts of her past and embrace the possibilities of a future she had once thought lost forever.

Ava's fingers trembled as she lifted the steaming mug of coffee to her lips, the rich aroma mingling with the scent of Lena's lavender perfume. She took a sip, the bittersweet liquid warming her from within, a temporary respite from the turmoil that churned in her heart.

"I saw Jamie at the wedding," Ava confessed, her voice barely above a whisper. "It was like stepping into a dream, a vision from another life. All the memories, the feelings I thought I had buried, came rushing back in an instant."

Lena leaned forward, her elbows resting on the table, her eyes never leaving Ava's face. "The heart remembers, even when the mind tries to forget," she said softly, her words a gentle caress against Ava's battered soul.

Ava's gaze drifted to the window, the bustling street beyond a blur of colors and shapes. "I thought I had moved on, that I had found peace in the solitude of my work. But seeing Jamie again... it was like a revelation, a reminder of the love we once shared, the love I've been running from."

Lena reached across the table, her weathered hand covering Ava's, a silent gesture of support. "Fear is a powerful thing, Ava. It can make us doubt ourselves, doubt the very things that once brought us joy. But it's never too late to embrace the truth of your heart."

Ava's eyes glistened with unshed tears, the weight of

her emotions threatening to spill over. "I'm afraid, Lena. Afraid of opening myself up again, of risking the pain that comes with love. What if I'm not enough? What if I've lost my chance at happiness?"

Lena's grip tightened, her voice firm yet gentle. "You are enough, Ava. You always have been. And love, true love, is worth the risk. It's the very essence of life, the light that guides us through the darkness."

Ava's breath caught in her throat, the truth of Lena's words piercing through the veil of her fears. In that moment, she knew that she could no longer hide from the yearning that pulsed through her veins, the longing for a love that had never truly died.

Ava drew in a shaky breath, her gaze drifting to the window where the soft, golden light of the afternoon sun filtered through the lace curtains. The gentle hum of conversation and the aroma of freshly brewed coffee enveloped her, a comforting cocoon amidst the turbulence of her emotions.

"I want to fight for it, Lena," Ava whispered, her voice trembling with a newfound resolve. "I want to fight for the love Jamie and I once had, for the future we could build together."

Lena's eyes sparkled with warmth, a knowing smile playing at the corners of her lips. "Then fight, my dear. Fight with every fiber of your being. Don't let the shadows of the past dictate the brightness of your future."

Ava's heart swelled with a mix of fear and exhilaration, the prospect of confronting her past and embracing her true desires both terrifying and thrilling. She closed her eyes for a moment, picturing Jamie's face, the way her hazel eyes crinkled when she laughed, the softness of her touch that had once set Ava's soul ablaze.

"I'll reach out to her," Ava declared, her voice growing stronger with each word. "I'll tell her how I feel, how I've never stopped loving her, how I want to build a life together."

Lena nodded, pride shining in her eyes. "You have a beautiful heart, Ava. Don't be afraid to share it with the world, to let love guide you on this journey."

Ava's fingers curled around her coffee mug, the warmth seeping into her skin, a tangible reminder of the love and support that surrounded her. She knew that the path ahead would be filled with challenges, with moments of doubt and fear, but she also knew that she was no longer willing to let those fears control her destiny.

As the sunlight danced across the table, casting a golden glow on Lena's face, Ava felt a renewed sense of purpose, a determination to fight for the love she had once let slip through her fingers. She would face her past, confront her demons, and emerge stronger, ready to embrace the future that awaited her, a future where love reigned supreme.

Lena's gaze softened as she leaned forward, her voice a

soothing balm to Ava's racing thoughts. "Remember, Ava, love is a delicate dance. It requires patience, understanding, and a willingness to embrace vulnerability. As you and Jamie navigate this new chapter, be gentle with each other, and with yourselves."

Ava nodded, her eyes glistening with unshed tears. The weight of Lena's words settled upon her heart, a gentle reminder of the challenges that lay ahead. She knew that the road to reconciliation would be fraught with emotional landmines, the ghosts of their past threatening to resurface at every turn.

"How do I even begin?" Ava whispered, her voice trembling with uncertainty. "It's been so long, and we've both changed. What if she doesn't feel the same way anymore? What if—why if its only physical attraction and she's not willing to commit? I don't want to risk being hurt again."

Lena reached across the table, her weathered hand resting atop Ava's, a gesture of comfort and reassurance. "Start with honesty, Ava. Speak from your heart. Whether it's through a heartfelt letter or a face-to-face conversation, let your words be a reflection of your truth."

Ava's mind raced with possibilities, each scenario playing out like a scene from one of her plays. She could pour her soul onto paper, crafting a love letter that would rival the greatest works of literature. Or she could gather

her courage and seek out Jamie in person, risking the rawness of an unscripted encounter.

As if sensing her inner turmoil, Lena continued, "There's no right or wrong way, Ava. Trust your instincts, and let your love guide you. Jamie deserves to know the depth of your feelings, the sincerity of your intentions."

Ava's gaze drifted to the window, the bustling street outside a blur of activity. She imagined herself standing before Jamie, her heart laid bare, the words she had held back for so long finally spilling forth. The thought was both terrifying and exhilarating, a leap of faith into the unknown.

"I think I need to spent time with her," Ava murmured, her decision solidifying with each passing moment. "I need to look into her eyes and tell her every-thing I've been too afraid to say. I need to know if there's still a chance for us, if our love can withstand the test of time."

Lena smiled, a knowing twinkle in her eye. "Then go to her, Ava. Embrace the uncertainty, and trust in the power of your love. No matter the outcome, you'll have the peace of knowing you followed your heart."

Ava's heart swelled with gratitude, the warmth of Lena's support enveloping her like a comforting embrace. She knew that the path ahead would be filled with moments of doubt and fear, but she also knew that she was no longer alone in her journey.

As the sun dipped lower in the sky, casting a rosy glow across the coffee shop, Ava felt a renewed sense of purpose, a determination to fight for the love she had once let slip through her fingers. She would face her past, confront her demons, and emerge stronger, ready to embrace the future that awaited her, a future where love reigned supreme.

Ava reached across the table, clasping Lena's weathered hand in her own, her eyes glistening with unshed tears. "Thank you, Lena," she whispered, her voice trembling with emotion. "I don't know what I would do without your guidance and support. You've been a beacon of light in my darkest moments."

Lena's smile softened, her eyes reflecting the depth of her affection for the young woman before her. "You have a strength within you, Ava, a resilience that will carry you through any storm. Never forget that. And remember, I'm always here for you, ready to listen and offer comfort whenever you need it."

As Ava nodded, a wave of determination washing over her, the tinkling of the coffee shop's bell drew her attention to the entrance. There, framed by the soft glow of the afternoon sun, stood Toby, a knowing smile playing on his lips as he made his way towards their table.

"Well, well, if it isn't my favorite sister and our beloved

Lena," he teased, his voice warm with affection. "I hope I'm not interrupting anything important."

Ava shook her head, a smile tugging at the corners of her mouth. "You're always welcome, Toby. In fact, your timing couldn't be more perfect.

Toby raised an eyebrow, curiosity piqued as he slid into the empty chair beside Lena. "Oh? Do tell."

Lena chuckled softly, her eyes twinkling with mirth. "Our dear Ava has made a decision, one that requires a great deal of courage and faith."

Toby's gaze shifted to his sister, his expression softening as he recognized the determination in her eyes. "Let me guess, you're going to reach out to Jamie?"

Ava nodded, her heart fluttering at the mere mention of Jamie's name. "I can't let fear control my life any longer, Toby. I need to confront our past, to tell her how I truly feel."

Toby reached across the table, his hand finding Ava's, his touch a reassuring presence. "I'm proud of you, Ava. It takes a brave soul to face their fears head-on. And know that no matter what happens, I'll be right here, supporting you every step of the way."

As the three of them sat in the cozy confines of the coffee shop, their hands intertwined in a silent show of solidarity, Ava felt a warmth spread through her chest, a sense of belonging and love that she had been searching for all her life. With Lena and Toby by her side, she knew that she could face anything, even the uncertain future that lay ahead.

The sun dipped below the horizon, painting the sky in a symphony of oranges and pinks, as Ava's mind wandered to Jamie, to the love they had once shared, and to the possibility of a second chance. She knew that the road ahead would be filled with challenges, but for the first time in years, she felt ready to face them, armed with the unwavering support of those who loved her most.

Ava stood up from the table, her eyes glistening with a newfound determination. The soft clinking of coffee cups and the gentle hum of conversation faded into the background as she focused on the path ahead. She turned to Lena and Toby, a grateful smile gracing her lips. "Thank you both, for everything. I don't know what I'd do without you."

Lena reached out, her warm hand gently squeezing Ava's arm. "You're stronger than you know, my dear. Trust in yourself and the love you carry in your heart."

Toby nodded, his voice filled with conviction. "Remember, Ava, love is a risk worth taking. I've learned that lesson the hard way, but it's one that has guided me ever since. When you find that special someone who makes your heart sing, you hold on tight and never let go."

Ava drew in a deep breath, letting their words wash over her like a soothing balm. As she made her way out of the coffee shop, the cool evening breeze caressed her face, carrying with it the scent of blooming jasmine and the promise of new beginnings. Ava's footsteps echoed on the sidewalk, each one a testament to the courage she had found within herself.

The city streets stretched out before her, a labyrinth of possibilities and uncertainties. Yet, amidst the chaos, Ava's mind was clear, her purpose unwavering. With each step, Ava felt the weight of her fears and doubts falling away, replaced by a fierce determination to fight for the love she deserved.

As the city lights flickered to life, casting a soft glow on the streets, Ava's heart swelled with a sense of hope and anticipation.

And so, with a smile on her face and a fire in her heart, Ava walked on, ready to embrace the future and all the possibilities it held. The night air whispered its secrets, and the stars above twinkled with the promise of a love that would never fade, a love that would endure through the ages, a love that would always find its way home.

Six

AVA STEPPED into the quaint café, a rush of warm air and the rich aroma of coffee beans enveloping her. Her heart fluttered with anticipation as her eyes scanned the room, searching for the one person who could make everything else fade away. And there she was, tucked away in a corner table, her hazel eyes already locked on Ava's.

Jamie rose from her seat, a radiant smile illuminating her face as she moved towards Ava with purposeful strides. In a heartbeat, they were in each other's arms, holding on tightly as if making up for all the days they had been apart. Ava breathed in Jamie's familiar scent, a mix of lavender and old books, and felt the weight of the world lift from her shoulders.

"I've missed you so much," Jamie whispered, her breath warm against Ava's ear.

"Not nearly as much as I've missed you," Ava replied, reluctantly pulling back to gaze into Jamie's eyes. In them, she saw a reflection of her own longing, a testament to the bond they shared.

Hand in hand, they made their way to the corner table, their fingers intertwined in a subtle yet powerful display of affection. As they settled into their seats, Ava couldn't help but notice the curious glances from the other patrons. Their eyes lingered on the two women, some filled with intrigue, others with a hint of disapproval.

Ava's heart tightened, a familiar pang of unease settling in her chest. She knew all too well the judgment that came with loving someone society deemed "inappropriate." The scars from her past relationship still ached, reminding her of the pain that came with defying conventions.

But as she looked across the table at Jamie, with her warm smile and gentle eyes, Ava felt a surge of defiance. Their love was real, and it deserved to be celebrated, not hidden away in the shadows. She reached for Jamie's hand, needing to feel the reassuring touch of her skin.

"Let them stare," Ava said quietly, her voice laced with determination. "I'm done hiding how I feel about you."

Jamie's eyes widened, a flicker of surprise giving way to a tender smile. "Ava Sinclair, you never cease to amaze me.

Your strength, your passion...it's one of the many reasons I fell in love with you."

Ava's heart swelled at Jamie's words, a blush creeping into her cheeks. In that moment, surrounded by the soft chatter of the café and the warmth of Jamie's presence, everything else seemed to fade away. The curious glances, the lingering doubts...none of it mattered. All that existed was the love they shared, burning bright and unapologetic.

* * *

Ava traced her fingers along the lines of Jamie's palm, savoring the familiar contours of her skin. "Do you remember the first time we met?" she asked softly, a nostalgic smile playing on her lips.

Jamie's eyes sparkled with the memory. "How could I forget? You walked into my classroom, all confidence and charm, and I knew right then that you were going to turn my world upside down."

Laughter bubbled up in Ava's throat, a welcome release from the tension that had settled in her chest. "I was a nervous wreck that day," she admitted, shaking her head. "But there was something about you, Jamie...something that made me feel like I could be myself, no matter what."

Jamie's gaze softened, a tender expression washing

over her features. "You've always been authentic, Ava. It's one of the things I admire most about you. The way you pour your heart into your work, the way you fight for what you believe in...it's inspiring."

Ava felt a warmth spreading through her chest, a sense of acceptance and understanding that she had craved for so long. With Jamie, she could let down her walls, revealing the vulnerabilities that she kept hidden from the world.

But even as they lost themselves in the comfort of shared memories, the weight of societal expectations lingered in the air. Ava could feel it, like a shadow at the edges of their happiness, threatening to eclipse the light they had found in each other.

She glanced around the café, taking in the curious stares and whispered conversations. A part of her wanted to shrink away, to retreat into the safety of secrecy. But a stronger part of her, the part that had been forged in the fires of adversity, refused to back down.

"Jamie," Ava said, her voice low and intense, "I know this isn't going to be easy. People will talk, they'll judge us for loving each other. But I'm ready to face whatever comes our way, as long as I have you by my side."

Jamie's hand tightened around Ava's, a silent promise of support and unwavering love. "Together," she murmured, her hazel eyes shining with determination.

"We'll show the world that our love is just as valid, just as beautiful, as any other."

Ava nodded, a fierce pride swelling in her chest. They had fought too hard, overcome too much, to let the opinions of others dictate their happiness. Their love was a force to be reckoned with, a beacon of hope in a world that often seemed intent on tearing them down.

As they sat there, hands intertwined and hearts beating in unison, Ava knew that they were stronger than any obstacle that lay ahead. With Jamie by her side, she could face anything, secure in the knowledge that their love would always light the way.

The soft clink of a cup on a saucer drew Ava's attention away from Jamie's captivating gaze. From the corner of her eye, she noticed a familiar figure seated at a nearby table. Rebecca Thompson, Jamie's colleague, sat with her back ramrod straight, her piercing gray eyes fixed on the couple with an intensity that made Ava's skin prickle.

Jamie, sensing the shift in Ava's demeanor, followed her gaze. A flicker of recognition crossed her features, followed by a flash of apprehension. "That's Rebecca," she murmured, her voice tinged with a mix of resignation and unease. "She's always been... critical of our relationship."

Ava's heart clenched at the weariness in Jamie's tone.

How many times had her love been forced to endure the judgment and scrutiny of others, simply for daring to follow her heart? A surge of protectiveness welled up within her, mingling with a simmering anger at the narrow-mindedness that still persisted in their world.

But even as the weight of Rebecca's disapproving stare bore down upon them, Ava refused to let it shatter the fragile bubble of intimacy they had created. She leaned in closer to Jamie, the warmth of her breath ghosting across her lover's cheek as she whispered, "Let her stare. She can't touch what we have, Jamie. Our love is stronger than her prejudice."

Jamie's eyes softened, a tender smile tugging at the corners of her lips. "You're right," she breathed, her fingers tightening around Ava's in a gesture of solidarity. "I've spent so long hiding, trying to fit into a mold that was never meant for me. But with you, I feel like I can finally be myself, without fear or shame."

Ava's heart swelled with love and pride. She knew all too well the courage it took to defy societal expectations, to risk the judgment and rejection of those around you for the sake of authenticity. Jamie's bravery, her willingness to stand firm in the face of adversity, only made Ava love her more.

As they sat there, their voices hushed and intimate, Ava allowed herself to dream of a future where their love would be celebrated, not condemned. A future where they could walk hand in hand without fear, where their relationship would be seen as a source of inspiration, rather than a target for scorn.

But even as she dared to hope, Ava knew that the road ahead would be fraught with challenges. Rebecca's presence, her silent condemnation, was just a taste of the obstacles they would face. The world was not always kind to those who dared to love differently.

And yet, as Ava gazed into Jamie's eyes, she saw a strength and resilience that took her breath away. Together, they would weather any storm, face any adversity, and emerge all the stronger for it. Their love was a force to be reckoned with, a light that would pierce through the darkest of shadows.

With a soft smile, Ava leaned in and pressed a gentle kiss to Jamie's lips, pouring all of her love and devotion into the simple gesture. "We've got this," she whispered, her forehead resting against Jamie's. "Together, we can face anything."

Rebecca's sharp voice cut through the intimate moment like a knife, shattering the fragile peace that had settled over Ava and Jamie's table. "Well, well, well," she drawled, her lips curling into a sneer as she loomed over them. "Isn't this cozy?"

Ava's heart clenched, a sickening mixture of dread and anger churning in her stomach as she slowly turned to face their intruder. Rebecca's gray eyes glittered with malice, her perfectly manicured fingers tapping an ominous rhythm against her folded arms.

"Rebecca," Jamie said, her voice tight with barely restrained frustration. "Can we help you with something?"

"Oh, I don't know," Rebecca replied, her tone dripping with mock innocence. "I was just wondering if you two had given any thought to the example you're setting for your students. A teacher and a playwright, carrying on like a couple of lovesick teenagers in public? It's hardly appropriate, is it?"

Ava's blood boiled, a searing heat rising in her cheeks as she fought to maintain her composure. How dare this woman, this stranger, presume to judge them? To cast aspersions on the purity and beauty of their love?

"I don't see how our relationship is any of your concern," Ava said, her voice low and dangerous. "Jamie and I are both consenting adults, and what we do in our private lives has no bearing on our professional roles."

Rebecca scoffed, her lips twisting into a cruel smirk. "Private lives? Please. You two are practically putting on a show for the whole café. It's indecent, is what it is. And as for your 'professional roles'... well, let's just say that some of us have higher standards than others."

Ava's hand clenched into a fist beneath the table, her

nails biting into her palm as she struggled to rein in her temper. She wanted nothing more than to lash out, to put this spiteful woman in her place with a few well-chosen words. But she knew that rising to the bait would only make things worse.

Instead, she took a deep, steadying breath, fixing Rebecca with a steely gaze. "I'm sorry you feel that way," she said, her voice cold and unyielding. "But your opinion, frankly, means very little to me. Jamie and I love each other, and that love is not up for debate or judgment. Not from you, not from anyone."

Rebecca's eyes narrowed, a flicker of surprise and anger crossing her features before she quickly masked it with a sneer. "Love?" she scoffed. "Please. This is nothing more than a tawdry little fling, a momentary lapse in judgment. Sooner or later, you'll both come to your senses and realize how foolish you're being."

Ava's heart hammered in her chest, a white-hot rage coursing through her veins. She opened her mouth to retort, to put this vicious harpy in her place once and for all—

But before she could speak, Jamie's hand found hers beneath the table, their fingers intertwining in a silent show of support and solidarity. Ava glanced over at her love, seeing the quiet strength and determination shining in her eyes.

"Rebecca," Jamie said, her voice calm but firm. "I

think it's time for you to leave. Ava and I have nothing more to say to you."

For a moment, Rebecca looked as though she might argue. But something in Jamie's expression must have given her pause, because she simply huffed out a breath and spun on her heel, stalking away from their table with her head held high.

Ava watched her go, her heart still racing with the aftermath of their confrontation. She knew that this was only the beginning, that there would be many more Rebeccas in their future, many more narrow-minded people who would seek to tear them down and undermine their love.

But as she turned back to Jamie, seeing the love and devotion shining in her eyes, Ava knew that they would face those challenges together. Their love was a force to be reckoned with, a bond that could not be broken by the petty judgments and prejudices of others.

"I love you," she whispered, bringing their joined hands to her lips and pressing a soft kiss to Jamie's knuckles. "No matter what anyone else says or thinks, I will always love you."

Jamie smiled, her eyes glistening with unshed tears. "I love you too, Ava. Always and forever."

And in that moment, as the rest of the world fell away and only the truth of their love remained, Ava knew that they could face anything, as long as they had each other.

* * *

The hushed whispers and furtive glances of the other café patrons seemed to fade into the background as Ava lost herself in the depths of Jamie's hazel eyes. In that moment, it was as if they were the only two people in the world, their love a cocoon that shielded them from the harsh realities of judgment and intolerance.

But even as they basked in the glow of their shared devotion, Ava could feel the weight of the stares boring into her back, the unspoken condemnation that hung heavy in the air. She knew that they couldn't stay here forever, that they would have to face the world outside and all the challenges that came with it.

With a sigh, she reluctantly pulled her hand away from Jamie's, already missing the warmth and comfort of her touch. "We should probably go," she murmured, her voice low and tinged with regret. "I don't want to cause any more of a scene."

Jamie nodded, her eyes shadowed with understanding. "You're right. Let's get out of here."

As they stood to leave, Ava couldn't help but notice the way the other patrons' gazes followed them, some curious, some disapproving, and some outright hostile. She squared her shoulders, determined not to let their judgment get to her, but she could feel the tension coiling in her gut, the unease that came with being the subject of so much unwanted attention.

They made their way to the door, the bell above it jingling cheerfully as they stepped out into the bright sunlight. The fresh air was a welcome relief after the stifling atmosphere of the café, and Ava took a deep breath, letting it out slowly as she tried to calm her racing heart.

Jamie's hand found hers again, their fingers inter-twining as they started down the sidewalk. "Are you okay?" she asked softly, her voice laced with concern.

Ava nodded, managing a small smile. "I will be. It's just... hard, sometimes. Dealing with people like Rebecca, knowing that there will always be someone waiting to tear us down."

"I know," Jamie said, her grip tightening on Ava's hand. "But we can't let them win, Ava. We can't let their hatred and bigotry dictate how we live our lives."

Ava knew she was right, but it was easier said than done. The weight of societal expectations and judgment could be crushing at times, and she wondered if they would ever truly be free of it.

As if sensing her thoughts, Jamie stopped walking, turning to face Ava with a fierce determination in her eyes. "Listen to me," she said, her voice low and intense. "I love you, Ava Sinclair. I love you with every fiber of my being, and nothing and no one will ever change that. Not Rebecca, not anyone else who tries to stand in our way."

Ava felt tears prick at the corners of her eyes, overwhelmed by the depth of emotion in Jamie's words. "I love you too," she whispered, her voice cracking with the weight of it all. "More than anything."

Jamie smiled, a soft, tender thing that made Ava's heart ache with love. "Then that's all that matters," she said, reaching up to brush a stray lock of hair from Ava's face. "As long as we have each other, we can face anything."

And as they stood there on the sidewalk, the world passing by around them, Ava knew that she was right. Their love was a force to be reckoned with, a bond that could weather any storm. And no matter what challenges lay ahead, they would face them together, hand in hand, heart to heart.

Hand in hand, Ava and Jamie walked down the street, their footsteps falling in perfect sync as they put distance between themselves and the café. The weight of their defiance hung in the air around them, a tangible presence that seemed to crackle with energy. Ava could still feel the adrenaline coursing through her veins, the rush of standing up for their love in the face of judgment and prejudice.

As they turned the corner, Jamie pulled Ava to a stop, her hazel eyes searching Ava's face with a mix of concern and admiration. "Are you okay?" she asked softly, her hand reaching up to brush a stray lock of hair from Ava's forehead.

Ava leaned into the touch, her eyes fluttering closed for a moment as she savored the warmth of Jamie's skin against her own. "I am now," she murmured, a small smile tugging at the corners of her mouth. "I'm just sorry you had to go through that, Jamie. I know how much you value your privacy."

Jamie shook her head, her gaze fierce with determination. "No, Ava. I'm not sorry. I'm proud of you, of us. What we have is special, and I won't let anyone make me feel ashamed of it."

Ava's heart swelled with love and gratitude, and she pulled Jamie in for a tender kiss, not caring who might see them. As their lips met, Ava felt a sense of rightness settle over her, a deep certainty that this was where she was meant to be.

When they finally pulled apart, Ava rested her forehead against Jamie's, their breath mingling in the scant space between them. "I love you, Jamie Hawthorne," she whispered, her voice thick with emotion. "And I'm not going to let anything or anyone come between us. Not even the ghosts of our past."

Jamie's eyes glistened with unshed tears, and she nodded, her hand tightening around Ava's. "I love you too, Ava Sinclair. And I'm with you, every step of the way. No matter what the future holds."

As they stood there, wrapped in each other's arms, Ava felt a sense of hope and possibility suffuse her being. They had faced their fears and emerged stronger, more united than ever before. And whatever challenges lay ahead, Ava knew that with Jamie by her side, they could overcome anything.

The afternoon sun dappled the sidewalk as Ava and Jamie strolled hand in hand, their steps leisurely and unhurried. The confrontation in the café seemed to fade with each passing moment, replaced by a renewed sense of connection and understanding. Ava glanced at Jamie, admiring the way the golden light played across her features, highlighting the strength and beauty that had first drawn Ava to her.

Jamie squeezed Ava's hand, a gesture that spoke volumes without the need for words. They walked in comfortable silence, the sounds of the city a distant hum, until they reached a secluded park bench nestled beneath a sprawling oak tree. Jamie tugged Ava down beside her, their thighs pressing together as they settled onto the sun-warmed wood.

Ava leaned her head on Jamie's shoulder, breathing in the familiar scent of her perfume mingled with the earthy aroma of the park. "I'm sorry," she murmured, her voice barely above a whisper. "For letting Rebecca get to me, for doubting us, even for a moment."

Jamie turned, her hazel eyes searching Ava's face with a tender intensity that made Ava's heart skip a beat. "You have nothing to apologize for, love. We both have our scars, our fears. But they don't define us, and they certainly don't define what we have together."

Ava nodded, a lump forming in her throat as she traced the delicate lines of Jamie's face with her fingertips. *How did I get so lucky?* she wondered, marveling at the depth of love and understanding she saw reflected in Jamie's eyes. *To have found someone who sees me, all of me, and still chooses to love me, unconditionally.*

Jamie leaned into Ava's touch, her eyes fluttering closed for a moment as she savored the sensation. When she opened them again, they were bright with a fierce determination. "I meant what I said back there, Ava. I'm in this, with you, no matter what. And I won't let anyone, not even the ghosts of our pasts, come between us."

Ava felt a rush of emotion, a heady mix of love and gratitude and relief, and she surged forward, capturing Jamie's lips in a searing kiss. Jamie responded instantly, her hands tangling in Ava's hair as she deepened the kiss, pouring all of her love and passion into the embrace.

When they finally broke apart, breathless and flushed, Ava rested her forehead against Jamie's, a smile playing at the corners of her mouth. "I love you, Jamie Hawthorne. More than I ever thought possible."

Jamie grinned, her eyes sparkling with mischief and adoration. "And I love you, Ava Sinclair. Forever and always."

As they stayed there, wrapped in each other's arms, the world seemed to fall away, leaving only the two of them, their love a shining beacon in the face of all the challenges that lay ahead. And Ava knew, with a certainty that settled deep in her bones, that together, they could weather any storm, overcome any obstacle, and build a future filled with joy, laughter, and endless love.

Ava felt the cooling air hit her skin, making her shiver slightly. She was drunk and high on the rush of love, her heart racing with anticipation.

"Come home with me," Jamie purred, her eyes locked onto Ava's as she took a step closer. "Or, invite me home with you."

Ava smiled coyly, her breath catching in her throat at Jamie's proximity. "I couldn't without being more certain of where thin is heading," she replied, leaning into Jamie's warm embrace.

Their bodies pressed tightly together as they shared a lingering kiss that left them both panting for more. Without breaking apart, Jamie reached behind Ava and grabbed her ass cheek firmly before pulling her closer still so that their hips were grinding against each other in an erotic dance of seduction.

Desire coursed through Ava's veins as she savored this moment of intimacy with another woman for the first time—feeling wanted and needed like never before. "I think we should take this somewhere more private," Jamie whispered hoarsely into Ava's ear while trailing hot kisses down her neckline towards her breasts. "Go get in your car and follow me."

Without hesitation or question, Ava obeyed. Finding her car in the carpark, driving near Jamie's car, then following, shutting out everything else from her mind but each other. Jamie drove.

Ava trailed behind as they journeyed to Jamie's private destination. They eagerly crawled into the backseat of Jamie's car, leaving the outside world behind and focusing solely on each other.

Their lips met again hungrily as their hands roamed freely over supple bodies covered in lace lingerie; teasingly stroking skin until it burned with passionate desire, both from expressing fully what was building up inside them; an intense need fueled by raw lust that consumed every fiber within them. But more than that, both irrevocably bound now forevermore intertwined as one soul connected through multiple orgasms experienced simultaneously throughout this beautifully erotic encounter...

Seven

THE NEON SIGN above the door bathed the sidewalk in a soft red glow, the name "The Scarlet Room" illuminated in elegant script. Ava stood before the entrance, her heart fluttering with a mix of anticipation and trepidation. She smoothed the front of her black dress, the silky fabric clinging to her curves in all the right places. Taking a deep breath, she pushed open the heavy wooden door and stepped inside.

The bar hummed with energy, the air thick with the mingling scents of whiskey and perfume. Laughter and animated chatter drifted from the various booths and tables scattered throughout the dimly lit space. Ava scanned the room, searching for a familiar face amidst the sea of strangers.

Her eyes landed on Jamie, perched on a barstool near

the back, a glass of amber liquid cradled between her slender fingers. As if sensing Ava's presence, Jamie turned, their gazes locking across the room. A slow smile spread across Jamie's lips, and she raised her glass in a silent toast of invitation.

Ava wove her way through the crowd, the click of her heels against the hardwood floor drowned out by the pulsing beat of the music. As she drew closer, she couldn't help but admire the way Jamie's emerald green blouse complemented her hazel eyes, or how a few stray curls had escaped her usually tidy updo to frame her face in soft tendrils.

"Hey you," Jamie murmured as Ava slid onto the stool beside her. "I'm so glad you could make it."

"I wouldn't miss it," Ava replied, hoping her voice didn't betray the nerves fluttering in her stomach. "Thanks for inviting me."

Jamie signaled the bartender for another drink before turning back to Ava with a warm smile. "I figured it was about time you met some of my friends. They're a great group - I think you'll really like them."

Ava nodded, trying to ignore the way her skin tingled where Jamie's knee brushed against her own beneath the bar. She fought the urge to reach out and tuck one of those errant curls behind Jamie's ear, to let her fingers linger against the soft skin of her cheek.

Focus, Ava, she chided herself silently. *You're here as a friend, nothing more.*

But as Jamie launched into a story about her day, her eyes sparkling with mirth and her laughter infectious, Ava couldn't help but wonder if acting, "just friends," in front of Jamie's friends, would ever be enough. Not when every fiber of her being ached to pull Jamie close and capture those smiling lips with her own.

She forced herself to concentrate on Jamie's words, to laugh in all the right places and nod along attentively. But beneath the surface, desire simmered like a slumbering beast, waiting for the moment to rise up and consume her whole.

As Jamie finished her story, a vibrant voice cut through the chatter of the bar. "Jamie, darling! There you are!"

Ava turned to see a striking woman with strawberry blonde hair and sparkling blue eyes approaching their table. The newcomer enveloped Jamie in an enthusiastic hug, her laughter ringing out like wind chimes in a summer breeze.

"And who might this enchanting creature be?" the woman asked, turning her attention to Ava with a dazzling smile.

"Miranda, this is Ava Sinclair," Jamie introduced, her hand coming to rest on the small of Ava's back. The touch, though innocent, sent a shiver racing down Ava's spine. "Ava, meet Miranda Foster, one of my dearest friends and the most talented event planner in town."

Miranda swept Ava into a warm embrace, the scent of her perfume—a heady mix of jasmine and vanilla—enveloping Ava like a sweet mist. "It's an absolute pleasure to meet you, Ava," Miranda said, her voice rich with genuine affection. "I've heard so much about you from Jamie."

Ava's heart skipped a beat at the thought of Jamie discussing her with her friends. She wondered what stories Jamie had shared, what details she had chosen to divulge.

"All good things, I hope," Ava replied, a playful lilt to her voice masking the uncertainty that coiled in her gut.

Miranda's laughter was a balm to Ava's frayed nerves. "Oh, honey, you have no idea." She winked conspiratorially at Jamie, who ducked her head, a pretty blush staining her cheeks.

As more of Jamie's friends joined their group, Ava found herself drawn into a whirlwind of conversations. They asked about her plays, her inspirations, her dreams for the future. And as she spoke, Ava felt a sense of connection, of kinship, blossoming like a tender shoot.

These were people who understood the fire that drove her, the passion that consumed her. They shared her love of the arts, her hunger for creation, her yearning for something more.

And through it all, Jamie remained a steady presence

at her side, their thighs pressed together beneath the table, their fingers brushing as they reached for their drinks. Each touch was a spark, a promise, a whispered secret that Ava longed to unravel.

As the night wore on and the laughter grew louder, Ava found herself leaning closer to Jamie, drawn in by the warmth of her smile and the gleam in her hazel eyes. And when Jamie's hand came to rest on her knee, fingertips tracing idle patterns against the fabric of her jeans, Ava's breath caught in her throat.

This is dangerous, a voice whispered in the back of her mind. *You're treading on thin ice, Ava Sinclair.*

But as Jamie threw her head back in laughter, her curls cascading down her back like a waterfall of silk, Ava knew that she was already lost. Lost in the depths of Jamie's eyes, in the curve of her smile, in the promise of what could be, yet confused about the relationship with Jamie. *Where do I fit in with Jamie's friends, especially Miranda?*

"I'd love to hear more about your creative process," Miranda said, her voice laced with enthusiasm. "How do you tap into those deep wells of emotion? How do you bring your characters to life with such authenticity?"

Ava paused, considering the question. It was a process she had never quite been able to put into words, a dance between instinct and craft, between the whispers of her heart and the discipline of her mind.

"It's a delicate balance," she began, her voice soft and

pensive. "I try to listen to my characters, to let them guide me through their stories. I draw from my own experiences, my own emotions, and then I shape them, mold them, until they take on a life of their own."

Miranda nodded, her expression one of rapt attention. "That's incredible. It's like you're channeling something greater than yourself, something almost... magical."

Ava smiled, a glimmer of understanding passing between them. "In a way, I suppose I am. Writing is my way of making sense of the world, of grappling with the big questions, the ones that keep me up at night."

"I know exactly what you mean," Miranda said, her eyes alight with a kindred passion. "It's the same for me with event planning. Each celebration, each gathering, is a chance to create something beautiful, something meaningful. A chance to bring people together and forge connections that last a lifetime."

They traded stories of their favorite plays, the books that had changed their lives, the moments of artistic revelation that had left them breathless.

And through it all, Ava felt a sense of kinship growing between them, a recognition of a shared passion, a shared understanding of the power of art to transform, to heal, to inspire.

She glanced over at Jamie, who was deep in conversation with another friend, her laughter ringing out above the din of the bar. And in that moment, Ava felt a rush of gratitude for this woman who had brought her here, who had opened the door to this new world of friendship and possibility.

Maybe this is what I've been missing, she thought, her heart swelling with a tentative hope. *Maybe this is what I've been searching for all along. A place to belong, a chance to be seen, to be understood.*

As the night wore on and the conversations flowed, Ava found herself letting go of the doubt that had plagued her for so long, the fear that she was unworthy of love, of happiness.

This is just the beginning, she thought, as she caught Jamie's eye across the table, a secret smile passing between them. *The beginning of something beautiful, something true. And for the first time in a long time, I'm ready to embrace it with open arms.*

As the laughter from a shared anecdote faded into a comfortable lull, one of Jamie's friends, a tall man with a warm smile, turned to Ava and Jamie. "You know, it's been a long time since I've seen Jamie this happy," he said, his eyes twinkling with affection. "I can tell that you two have something special."

Ava felt a blush creep up her neck, her heart fluttering at the unexpected acknowledgment. She glanced at Jamie, who was smiling softly, her hazel eyes filled with a tender warmth that made Ava's breath catch in her throat.

"Thank you," Ava managed to say, her voice slightly trembling with emotion. "Jamie... she means the world to me."

Jamie reached out, her hand finding Ava's beneath the table, their fingers intertwining in a silent gesture of unity. "Ava's my rock," Jamie said, her voice low and sincere. "She's been there for me through everything, even when I didn't deserve it."

Another friend, a woman with short, spiky hair and a mischievous grin, chimed in. "You both deserve all the happiness in the world," she said, raising her glass in a toast. "To Ava and Jamie, and to second chances!"

The group echoed the sentiment, their glasses clinking together in a chorus of support and acceptance. Ava felt a lump form in her throat, overwhelmed by the outpouring of love and understanding from these people who had been strangers mere hours ago.

Is this what it feels like? she wondered, her heart swelling with an unfamiliar sense of belonging. *To be part of something bigger than yourself, to be accepted for who you are, flaws and all?*

As the conversation flowed around her, Ava found herself stealing glances at Jamie, marveling at the way the soft light of the bar danced across her features, highlighting the curve of her cheek, the gentle slope of her nose. And in those stolen moments, she felt a sense of peace wash over her, a quiet certainty that this was exactly where she was meant to be.

With Jamie by my side, I feel like I can take on the world, Ava thought, a small smile tugging at the corners of her lips. *Together, we can face anything, overcome anything. And for the first time in my life, I'm not afraid to try.*

As the night wore on and the drinks flowed freely, Ava found herself drawn into a conversation with another of Jamie's friends, a petite blonde with a sharp tongue and a skeptical gaze. The woman leaned in close, her breath hot against Ava's ear as she spoke in a low, conspiratorial tone.

"So, you and Jamie, huh?" she said, her eyes narrowing slightly. "I hope you know what you're getting into. Jamie's been through a lot, and she doesn't need any more heartbreak."

Ava felt her heart skip a beat, a flicker of uncertainty crossing her features. But before she could respond, Miranda appeared at her side, her warm hand coming to rest on Ava's shoulder in a gesture of support.

"Now, now, Lila," Miranda chided gently, her voice soft but firm. "Ava and Jamie are both grown women, capable of making their own decisions. And from what I've seen, they bring out the best in each other."

Lila opened her mouth as if to argue, but something in Miranda's expression made her pause. After a moment, she shrugged, a rueful smile tugging at her lips.

"I suppose you're right," she conceded, her gaze softening as it shifted to Ava. "Just be good to her, okay? She deserves to be happy."

Ava nodded, a lump forming in her throat as she met Lila's gaze head-on. "I will," she promised, her voice barely above a whisper. "I swear it."

As Lila melted back into the crowd, Miranda gave Ava's shoulder a gentle squeeze, her eyes shining with warmth and understanding.

"Don't mind her," she murmured, her voice low and soothing. "She's just protective of Jamie, that's all. But I can see how much you care for each other, and that's all that matters."

Ava felt tears prick at the corners of her eyes, overwhelmed by the depth of Miranda's kindness and compassion. *How did I get so lucky?* she wondered, her heart swelling with gratitude. *To have found not just Jamie, but this whole amazing group of people who accept me for who I am?*

As if sensing her thoughts, Jamie appeared at her side, her fingers twining with Ava's beneath the table. "Everything okay?" she asked softly, her brow furrowed with concern.

Ava nodded, a watery smile spreading across her face as she leaned into Jamie's touch. "Everything's perfect," she whispered, her voice thick with emotion. "I just... I never thought I could have this, you know? Friends who support me, a woman who loves me... it's more than I ever dared to hope for."

Jamie's eyes shone with unshed tears as she lifted Ava's hand to her lips, pressing a soft kiss to her knuckles. "You deserve all of this and more," she murmured, her voice fierce with conviction. "And I promise, I'll spend every day of my life making sure you know just how loved and cherished you are."

As the night wore on and the laughter and conversation flowed around them, Ava and Jamie clung to each other, their hearts full to bursting with the knowledge that they were not alone. That they had each other, and a whole community of people who loved and supported them, no matter what challenges lay ahead.

They played trivia, the competitive spirit in the room grew, with friendly banter and playful jabs exchanged between the teams. Ava found herself caught up in the excitement, her quick wit and extensive knowledge of literature and the arts proving invaluable to her team. She reveled in the camaraderie, the sense of belonging that had eluded her for so long.

Amidst the lively atmosphere, Ava's gaze kept drifting to Jamie, drawn to her like a moth to a flame. The soft glow of the overhead lights cast a warm halo around

Jamie's face, highlighting the delicate curve of her cheekbones and the sparkle in her hazel eyes. Ava's heart fluttered each time their eyes met, a secret language passing between them in the briefest of glances.

Jamie, too, found it difficult to keep her attention on the game, her mind preoccupied with the woman beside her. She marveled at the way Ava seamlessly navigated the social interaction, her confidence and charm shining through in every word and gesture. It was a side of Ava that Jamie had never seen before, and she found herself falling even deeper under her spell.

As the final round of the trivia game approached, Ava and Jamie's team found themselves neck and neck with their opponents. The tension in the room was palpable, broken only by the occasional burst of laughter or good-natured groan. Ava leaned forward, her brow furrowed in concentration as she listened to the final question.

"In Shakespeare's 'Romeo and Juliet,' what is the name of the friar who marries the titular characters?"

Ava's hand shot up, a triumphant grin spreading across her face. "Friar Laurence!" she exclaimed, her voice ringing out clear and strong.

The room erupted in cheers as Ava's team was declared the winner, and Jamie pulled her into a tight hug, her face alight with pride. "You were amazing," she whispered, her breath hot against Ava's ear.

Ava shivered, the feeling of Jamie's body pressed

against hers igniting a fire in her veins. She pulled back slightly, her eyes locking with Jamie's in a heated gaze. In that moment, the rest of the world fell away, and all that existed was the two of them, lost in the depths of each other's eyes.

"Jamie, I..." Ava's voice trailed off, the words catching in her throat. There was so much she wanted to say, so much she needed Jamie to know. But before she could continue, Miranda's voice cut through the haze, pulling them back to reality.

"Alright, lovebirds, break it up," she teased, her eyes twinkling with mischief. "There'll be plenty of time for that later. For now, let's celebrate our victory!"

Ava and Jamie reluctantly pulled apart, their cheeks flushed and their hearts racing. As they joined their friends in a round of celebratory drinks, they couldn't help but steal glances at each other across the table, their fingers brushing together in fleeting touches that promised so much more.

As the laughter and chatter of their friends filled the air, Ava and Jamie again found themselves drawn to each other, their bodies gravitating closer as if pulled by an invisible force. Jamie's hand rested gently on Ava's knee beneath the table, her thumb tracing small circles that sent shivers up Ava's spine.

"I'm so glad you came tonight," Jamie whispered, her

breath warm against Ava's ear. "Having you here, with my friends, it feels... right."

Ava's heart swelled at Jamie's words, a sense of belonging washing over her. She laced her fingers through Jamie's, squeezing gently. "I wouldn't want to be anywhere else."

As the night drew to a close, the group slowly began to disperse, exchanging hugs and promises to meet again soon. Miranda pulled Ava into a tight embrace, her voice low and sincere. "Take care of her, Ava. She deserves all the happiness in the world."

Ava nodded, her throat tight with emotion. "I will. I promise."

Hand in hand, Ava and Jamie stepped out into the cool night air, the bustling sounds of the city enveloping them. They walked in comfortable silence, their shoulders brushing with each step, savoring the simple intimacy of being together.

Ava's mind wandered to the challenges that lay ahead—the whispers and judgments they would inevitably face. But as she glanced at Jamie, her profile illuminated by the soft glow of the streetlights, a fierce determination settled in her chest.

"Jamie," Ava said softly, tugging her to a stop. "I know this won't be easy. People will talk, they'll have opinions. But I want you to know that I'm in this, completely. You and me, together."

Jamie's eyes shimmered with unshed tears, a soft smile playing at the corners of her lips. She cupped Ava's face, her thumb brushing gently across her cheekbone. "Together," she echoed, her voice thick with emotion. "No matter what."

As their lips met in a tender kiss, Ava knew that this was a story of love, of courage, of two hearts entwined against all odds. And as they walked into the night, hand in hand, Ava felt a sense of peace wash over her, knowing that with Jamie by her side, she was ready to face whatever the future held.

Eight

AVA'S HEART raced as they walked, the closeness of Jamie's presence both comforting and unnerving. The years apart had done little to diminish the pull she felt towards her, the longing that ached in her bones. She glanced at Jamie, drinking in the sight of her profile, the way the wind tousled her short curls, the curve of her lips as she smiled at a passing thought.

The river came into view, its waters shimmering beneath the golden light. Memories flooded Ava's mind—stolen kisses by the water's edge, whispered promises under the stars, the bittersweet sting of goodbye. She swallowed past the lump in her throat, her fingers itching to reach out and take Jamie's hand, to feel the warmth of her skin against her own.

As they walked along the riverbank, the past and

present intertwining with each step, Ava knew that this moment was a crossroads. A chance to confront the ghosts that haunted them both, to reignite the love that had never truly died. She inhaled deeply, the autumn air filling her lungs, and turned to Jamie, ready to take the leap into the unknown.

Ava pointed to a weathered wooden bench nestled beneath a towering oak tree, its branches stretching out over the river. "Remember that bench?" she asked, a wistful smile playing on her lips. "We used to sit there for hours, dreaming about the future, about the lives we wanted to build together."

Jamie's eyes softened, a flicker of recognition dancing within their depths. "How could I forget? It was our special place, a sanctuary away from the world." She chuckled, a hint of mischief in her voice. "Remember when we got caught in that sudden downpour? We were soaked to the bone, but we couldn't stop laughing."

Laughter bubbled up from Ava's chest, the memory vivid and precious. "We ran for cover under that tree, huddling together for warmth. I remember the way you looked at me then, like I was the only person in the world."

They approached the bench, the years melting away with each step. Ava's heart raced, a heady mix of anticipation and trepidation coursing through her veins. She yearned to reach out, to bridge the distance between them, but a flicker of doubt held her back. What if too much time had passed? What if the love they once shared had faded like the autumn leaves?

"Let's sit for a while," Ava suggested, her voice soft and inviting. "Take a moment to breathe in the peace of this place."

Jamie nodded, a flicker of understanding in her eyes. They settled onto the bench, their shoulders brushing, a whisper of electricity sparking between them. Ava's skin tingled at the contact, a rush of warmth spreading through her body. She closed her eyes, letting the gentle breeze caress her face, the sound of the river a soothing melody in her ears.

In that moment, sitting beside Jamie, the weight of the past seemed to lift, replaced by a glimmer of hope, a promise of a future yet unwritten. Ava's heart swelled with love, with the realization that their story was far from over. She turned to Jamie, her voice trembling with emotion, ready to bare her soul and lay her heart on the line.

"I have a dream," Jamie confessed, her voice trembling with emotion. "I want to make a difference in my students' lives, to inspire them the way you've always inspired me." She reached out, her fingers brushing against Ava's hand, a touch that ignited a spark deep within them both. "I want to show them that love, real love, can conquer anything."

Ava's heart raced, the connection between them growing stronger with each passing second.

As they sat there, surrounded by the beauty of the park, the river flowing steadily beside them, Ava and Jamie knew that their exploration had only just begun. They had rediscovered the love that had always been there, the love that had the power to inspire and transform. And with each passing moment, they fell deeper, the walls around their hearts crumbling, making way for a love that would stand the test of time.

Ava and Jamie wandered hand in hand through the charming streets of Riverbend, their hearts light and their spirits buoyed by the love they had rediscovered. The town seemed to come alive around them, as if sensing the magic that flowed between the two women. As they turned a corner, Ava's eyes widened, a gasp escaping her lips. There, nestled between two quaint storefronts, was an art gallery, its windows adorned with vibrant paintings that seemed to beckon them closer.

"Let's go inside," Ava suggested, a hint of excitement in her voice. Jamie nodded, a smile playing at the corners of her mouth, and together they stepped into the gallery, the door chiming softly behind them.

The gallery was a feast for the senses, each wall adorned with artwork that spoke to the soul. Ava and Jamie moved slowly through the space, their hands still intertwined, as they took in the beauty that surrounded them. They paused before a large canvas, a swirl of colors that seemed to dance before their eyes, and Ava felt a sudden rush of emotion.

"It's like looking into my heart," she whispered, her voice thick with feeling. "The colors, the movement, it's like everything I've ever felt for you, captured in paint."

Jamie squeezed her hand, a silent acknowledgment of the depth of Ava's words. They stood there for a long moment, lost in the artwork and in each other, until the sound of a guitar drifted in from the street outside.

As they stepped out of the gallery, the music grew louder, a soulful melody that seemed to weave itself into the very fabric of the night. Ava's eyes sparkled, a playful grin spreading across her face as she tugged Jamie towards the sound. There, in a small open space, a street musician sat, his fingers dancing across the strings of his guitar, his eyes closed as he lost himself in the music.

Ava pulled Jamie close, her arms wrapping around her waist as they began to sway to the melody. The world around them faded away, until there was nothing but the music and the feel of each other's bodies, moving in perfect sync. Jamie leaned in, her forehead resting against Ava's, their breaths mingling in the cool night air.

As the music continued to play, Ava and Jamie lost themselves in the moment, their movements becoming more fluid, more sensual. Ava's hand slid up Jamie's back, her fingers tangling in her hair, as Jamie's lips brushed against her neck, sending shivers down her spine.

They danced until the music faded away, until the only sound was the beating of their hearts and the soft whispering of the wind. And when they finally stilled, their eyes locked, their lips parted, they knew that this was just the beginning. The beginning of a love story that would be told for years to come, a love story that would inspire and transform, just as their love had always done.

The sun's golden glow bathed the city in a warm embrace as Ava and Jamie strolled hand in hand through the bustling streets. Ava's eyes sparkled with a newfound excitement, her heart fluttering with the promise of what lay ahead. "I have an idea," she said, her voice tinged with a playful lilt. "Let's find a rooftop bar, somewhere we can watch the city come alive under the stars."

Jamie's face lit up, her hazel eyes reflecting the same sense of adventure. "Lead the way," she replied, giving Ava's hand a gentle squeeze.

Laughter and animated conversation filled the air as they navigated the city streets, their steps light and care-free. Ava couldn't help but marvel at the way Jamie's presence made even the most ordinary moments feel extraordinary, as if the world had suddenly been painted in vibrant hues.

As they approached the entrance of a trendy rooftop bar, the muted sounds of music and chatter drifted down to greet them. They ascended the stairs, each step building the anticipation within Ava's chest. When they finally stepped onto the rooftop, Ava's breath caught in her throat.

The cityscape stretched out before them, a glittering tapestry of lights that seemed to dance against the darkening sky. The gentle breeze carried the scent of blooming flowers and the distant hum of traffic, creating an atmosphere that was both exhilarating and intimate.

Ava led Jamie to the railing, their bodies instinctively drawing closer as they gazed out at the breathtaking view. The twinkling lights of the city below shimmered like a reflection of the stars above, and Ava felt a profound sense of connection to the world around her, to the woman beside her.

She turned to face Jamie, her heart swelling with a rush of emotion. "Thank you for today," Ava whispered, her voice raw with sincerity. "Being here with you, rediscovering our connection, it's been..." She paused, searching for the right words. "It's been everything I didn't know I needed."

Jamie's eyes softened, a tender smile playing on her lips. She reached out, gently brushing a stray lock of hair from Ava's face. "I feel the same way," she murmured, her fingertips lingering on Ava's cheek. "Being with you, it's like coming home."

Ava leaned into Jamie's touch, her eyes fluttering closed for a moment as she savored the warmth of her skin. When she opened them again, she found Jamie's gaze locked on hers, the intensity of her emotions reflected in the depths of her hazel eyes.

This is it, Ava thought, her heart pounding in her chest. *This is the moment I've been waiting for, the moment I've been dreaming of for so long.*

The air between them grew heavy with unspoken longing, the world around them fading into the background as they lost themselves in each other's eyes. Ava's breath hitched as Jamie leaned in closer, her lips parting slightly, an unspoken invitation hanging in the air between them.

Jamie's hand trembled slightly as she cupped Ava's face, her touch a soft caress against Ava's skin. "I've never stopped loving you, Ava," she confessed, her voice barely above a whisper. "All these years, the distance between us, it's only made my feelings for you grow stronger." She swallowed hard, her eyes glistening with unshed tears. "I know we've both been through so much, and I'm scared of getting hurt again, but I can't deny what's in my heart anymore."

Ava's breath caught in her throat, her heart racing at

Jamie's confession. She saw the vulnerability in Jamie's eyes, the raw honesty of her words, and it stirred something deep within her soul. "Jamie," she breathed, her voice thick with emotion. "I've never stopped loving you either. I've tried to move on, to bury my feelings, but they've always been there, waiting for this moment."

The city lights twinkled around them, casting a soft glow across their faces as they drew closer, the magnetic pull between them too strong to resist. Ava's hand found its way to the back of Jamie's neck, her fingers tangling in the soft curls at the nape of her neck. She could feel the warmth of Jamie's breath against her lips, the anticipation building in her veins.

Their lips met in a passionate kiss, the years of longing and desire pouring out of them in a single, perfect moment. Ava's senses were overwhelmed by the taste of Jamie's lips, the scent of her perfume, the feel of her body pressed against hers. It was a kiss that spoke of love, of healing, of a future filled with endless possibilities.

As they lost themselves in the kiss, the world around them faded away, the sounds of the city below muffled by the pounding of their hearts. Ava's hands roamed over Jamie's back, pulling her closer, desperate to feel every inch of her. She could feel the heat building between them, the desire that had been simmering beneath the surface for so long finally breaking free.

I never want this moment to end, Ava thought, her

mind hazy with passion. *I want to stay here forever, wrapped in Jamie's arms, lost in her kiss.*

And so they kissed, their bodies intertwined, their hearts beating as one, as the city lights continued to shine around them, a silent witness to the love that had never truly died.

Slowly, reluctantly, they pulled apart, their breaths mingling in the cool night air. Ava rested her forehead against Jamie's, her eyes still closed, savoring the lingering sensations of the kiss. When she finally opened them, she found Jamie gazing at her with a look of pure adoration, her eyes glistening with unshed tears.

"I love you," Jamie whispered, her voice raw with emotion. "I never stopped loving you, not for a single moment."

Ava's heart swelled at the words, a lump forming in her throat. "I love you too," she murmured, her fingers tracing the delicate contours of Jamie's face. "I'm so sorry for ever letting you go."

They stood there for a long moment, lost in each other's eyes, their smiles saying more than words ever could. It was a smile that spoke of forgiveness, of hope, of a love that had withstood the test of time.

Hand in hand, they wandered on. The streets of

Riverbend seemed to come alive around them, the colors more vibrant, the sounds more melodic. It was as if the world itself was celebrating their reunion, their love.

As they walked, they talked and laughed, their voices blending together in perfect harmony. They spoke of their dreams, their fears, their hopes for the future. They spoke of the challenges they knew they would face, the obstacles they would have to overcome. But they knew that together, they could handle anything.

We're stronger together, Ava mused, her hand tightening around Jamie's. *We always have been.*

* * *

When they finally reached Ava's home, they paused outside the door, their eyes meeting in a silent conversation. They knew that once they stepped inside, their reunion would be complete. They would be starting a new chapter in their lives, a chapter filled with love and laughter and endless possibilities.

But for now, they simply stood there, savoring the moment, the feeling of being in each other's presence once again. The scent of coffee and baked goods wafted out from the shop, mingling with the crisp night air, and Ava inhaled deeply, letting the familiar aroma wash over her.

This is home, she thought, her eyes drifting to the

warm glow of the windows. *This is where I belong, with Jamie by my side.*

And with that thought, they pushed open the door and stepped inside, ready to face whatever the future might bring, together.

Jamie's hand fitted perfectly in Ava's, their fingers intertwined, a physical manifestation of the bond they shared. Ava's thumb traced gentle circles on Jamie's skin, a silent reassurance that she was here, that this was real. The years of longing, of unspoken words and buried feelings, had led them to this moment, and Ava was determined to cherish every second.

"Ava," Jamie whispered, her voice a caress against the night air. Ava's heart clenched at the vulnerability in Jamie's words, the raw honesty that stripped away the layers of fear and doubt. She reached up, her fingers threading through Jamie's soft curls, drawing her closer until their foreheads touched.

"This is our reality now," Ava murmured, her breath mingling with Jamie's. "We've been given a second chance, and I'm not going to let it slip away. I love you, Jamie, and I'll fight for us, no matter what comes our way."

The words, spoken with such conviction, seemed to hang in the air between them, a vow that resonated deep within their souls. Jamie's lips found Ava's, a kiss that held the weight of a thousand unspoken promises, of love that had endured the test of time and circumstance.

"Let's not part again," Jamie said.

With a smile that held the brilliance of a thousand suns, Ava tugged Jamie closer, their bodies fitting together like puzzle pieces, perfectly aligned. The future stretching out before them, ripe with possibility and the promise of a love that would stand the test of time.

Ava's hand trembled as she traced the delicate line of Jamie's jaw, marveling at the softness of her skin, the warmth of her breath against her fingertips. How many times had she dreamed of this moment? How many nights had she lain awake, aching for the touch of Jamie's hand, the sweetness of her kiss?

Now, with scant inches separating them, the air between them fairly crackling with tension, every nerve ending in Ava's body sang with anticipation. She could feel the heat of Jamie's gaze, could see the rapid rise and fall of her chest, the flush of desire coloring her cheeks.

Slowly, tentatively, Jamie leaned forward, her eyelids fluttering closed.

Ava's heart seized in her chest, a sudden, desperate yearning overtaking her. She wanted this—wanted Jamie —with an intensity that bordered on feverish, an all-consuming need that set her very soul ablaze.

The first brush of Jamie's lips against her own was electric, a shock of sensation that rippled through Ava like wildfire. Soft and sweet and achingly tender, the kiss was a homecoming, a promise, a prayer—a shining beacon guiding her back to the safe harbor of Jamie's arms.

As the kiss deepened, Ava's world narrowed to the glorious press of Jamie's mouth against her own, the silken glide of Jamie's hair between her fingers, the intoxicating scent of her skin. Ava drank her in like a woman parched, each sweep of Jamie's tongue, each nip of her teeth, each breathy sigh stirring the embers of Ava's desire until she was certain she would be consumed by the flames.

Jamie's hands slid up Ava's back, pulling her closer, and Ava went willingly, every curve and hollow of her body molding perfectly to Jamie's. She could feel the thundering of Jamie's heartbeat, could taste the salt of tears on her lips—though whether they were Jamie's or her own, she couldn't be certain.

Time stretched and spun, seconds bleeding into minutes, minutes into hours, until Ava was drunk on the honeyed sweetness of Jamie's mouth, the velvet heat of her tongue. Nothing existed beyond this moment, this woman, this love that burned bright and fierce and eternal.

When at last they parted, Ava rested her forehead against Jamie's, their breath mingling in the sliver of space between them. "I love you," she whispered, her voice rough with emotion. "I've always loved you."

Jamie's eyes glittered with unshed tears, her smile tremulous but radiant. "I know," she murmured, tracing the curve of Ava's cheek with a reverent finger. "I've always known. Let's make our lives together from now on."

And as the sun dipped below the horizon, painting the sky in shades of gold and crimson, Ava and Jamie clung to each other, lost in the incandescent glow of a love that had endured the trials of time and distance, emerging stronger and more beautiful than ever before.

As the sun slipped below the horizon, painting the sky in shades of violet and indigo, Ava and Jamie sat in their secluded haven, their hearts laid bare, their hopes and dreams intertwining like the threads of a tapestry. The path ahead was uncertain, but one thing was clear: together, they could weather any storm, overcome any obstacle.

For in each other's arms, they had found a love that transcended time and circumstance. A love that had been tested, fractured, and reforged in the crucible of life's trials.

A love that would endure, now and always.

Ava's fingertips ghosted along the curve of Jamie's cheek, a feather-light caress that sent shivers cascading down Jamie's spine. The world around them faded away, the gentle rustling of leaves and the distant chirping of birds a mere whisper against the pounding of their hearts.

In the fading light, Jamie's hazel eyes glimmered with

an intensity that stole Ava's breath away. Those eyes—
once so familiar, now holding the promise of something
new, something precious and fragile and achingly
beautiful.

"Jamie," Ava breathed, her voice scarcely above a whisper. "There's so much I want to say, so much I—"

But Jamie silenced her with a look, a tender smile
playing at the corners of her mouth. "Shh," she
murmured, her lips a hairsbreadth from Ava's own. "I
know."

And she did. In that moment, suspended between
heartbeats, Jamie understood the words Ava couldn't give
voice to—the apologies and the regrets, the hopes and the
fears, the years of longing distilled into a single, perfect
instant.

Ava's fingers traced the delicate curve of Jamie's jaw,
marveling at the softness of her skin, the warmth that
seemed to radiate from her very core. In the fading light,
Jamie's hazel eyes glimmered with a depth of emotion that
stole Ava's breath, a kaleidoscope of love, longing, and
quiet contentment.

"I never thought I'd have this again," Jamie whispered,
her voice barely audible above the gentle rustling of leaves
in the breeze. "After everything that happened, I was so
sure I'd lost you forever."

Ava's heart clenched at the vulnerability in Jamie's
words, the echoes of past hurts that still lingered beneath

the surface. She brushed her thumb across Jamie's lower lip, a feather-light caress that held the weight of a thousand unspoken promises.

"You never lost me," Ava murmured, her gaze unwavering as she held Jamie's eyes with her own. "Even when we were apart, even when I thought I'd never see you again, you were always here." She pressed a hand to her heart, feeling the steady thrum beneath her palm. "You're a part of me, Jamie. You always have been, and you always will be."

Jamie's breath hitched, her eyes fluttering closed as she leaned into Ava's touch. In that moment, the years fell away, the pain and heartache fading to a distant memory as they lost themselves in the sheer perfection of their connection.

When Jamie's eyes opened once more, they shone with a fierce determination, a resolve that set Ava's soul ablaze. "I'm never letting you go again," she said, her voice low and fervent. "I don't care what anyone says, or what the world thinks. You're mine, Ava Sinclair. Now and forever."

Ava's heart soared at the declaration, the certainty in Jamie's words wrapping around her like a warm embrace. She knew, with a bone-deep certainty, that this was where she belonged—in the arms of the woman who had captured her heart so long ago, the woman who held the key to her every happiness.

As the last rays of sunlight painted the river in shades of molten gold, Ava and Jamie sealed their love with a kiss, a promise of forever whispered against each other's lips. The road ahead might be uncertain, but one thing was crystal clear—they would face whatever challenges lay ahead together, hand in hand, heart to heart, two souls entwined for all eternity.

Ava and Jamie stayed in their secluded spot a little longer, basking in the afterglow of their kiss, their fingers intertwined as they watched the sun dip below the horizon. The air around them seemed to shimmer with the intensity of their emotions, the world fading away until all that remained was the two of them, lost in the magic of the moment.

Ava's thumb traced gentle circles on the back of Jamie's hand, a silent promise of the love and devotion that flowed between them. She marveled at the way their bodies fit together so perfectly, as if they were two pieces of a puzzle, destined to be joined as one.

"I could stay here forever," Jamie murmured, her head resting on Ava's shoulder, her voice soft and dreamy. "Just you and me, watching the world go by."

Ava smiled, pressing a tender kiss to Jamie's forehead. "As tempting as that sounds, we both know we can't hide away forever. But I promise you, no matter what happens, I'll always be by your side."

Jamie lifted her head, her hazel eyes locking with Ava's

green ones, a flicker of uncertainty dancing in their depths. "You're sure about this? About us? I know it won't be easy, with the age difference and everything..."

Ava silenced her with a gentle finger to her lips. "I've never been more sure of anything in my life. You're the one I want, Jamie. The one I need. Nothing else matters."

As the last vestiges of daylight faded from the sky, Ava and Jamie reluctantly gathered their belongings and rose from the blanket, their steps now lighter and filled with a renewed sense of hope and possibility. They walked hand in hand along the riverbank, stealing glances and sharing secret smiles, their hearts full to bursting with the love they had found in each other's arms.

Hand in hand, Ava and Jamie continued their walk along the river, their footsteps falling into a synchronized rhythm as if they were two halves of a whole. The soft rustle of leaves and the gentle lapping of water against the shore provided a soothing backdrop to their newfound connection, a natural symphony that seemed to celebrate the love blossoming between them.

Ava glanced at Jamie, marveling at the way the fading light danced across her features, casting her in an almost ethereal glow. She squeezed Jamie's hand, savoring the warmth and comfort of her touch, a silent reassurance that this moment was real and not just a figment of her imagination.

Jamie turned to face Ava, a tender smile playing on her

lips. "I never thought I'd find this again," she murmured, her voice barely audible above the whisper of the wind. "After everything that happened, I was afraid to open my heart, but with you, it feels like coming home."

Ava's heart swelled at Jamie's words, a rush of emotion threatening to overwhelm her. She stopped walking and turned to face Jamie fully, her free hand reaching up to cradle her cheek. "I know exactly what you mean," she whispered, her thumb tracing the delicate curve of Jamie's jaw. "It's like all the pieces of my life have finally fallen into place, and I can breathe again."

They stood there for a long moment, lost in each other's eyes, the rest of the world fading away until it was just the two of them, cocooned in the magic of their connection. Ava leaned in, her lips brushing against Jamie's in a feather-light kiss, a promise of all the love and passion yet to come.

As they resumed their walk, Ava's mind wandered to the challenges that lay ahead. She knew that their relationship would not be without its obstacles, from the whispers and judgment of those who didn't understand to the internal battles they would both have to fight. But with Jamie by her side, Ava felt invincible, ready to take on anything that life threw their way.

The river stretched out before them, a shimmering ribbon of possibility, and Ava knew that this was just the beginning of their journey together. With every step, they were writing a new chapter in their story, a tale of love, hope, and the unbreakable bond between two souls who had found their way back to each other against all odds.

Throughout the rest of the night, they couldn't keep their eyes off each other, knowing what had happened between them in that car only intensified their connection. They danced together under the stars and shared kisses under hidden corners until eventually it was time to leave.

As they walked back to Ava's apartment, hand in hand.

Jamie entered Ava's wetness, their bodies merging in a passionate embrace. The air thick with the scent of arousal as they moved together in perfect rhythm, each touch more electric than the last. As the intensity built, their moans and cries echoed through the room until they reached a powerful climax, completely lost in each other's embrace. They had found love that knew no boundaries or inhibitions, only pure ecstasy and a fierce connection between two women who had surrendered to their deepest desires.